A Pocket Full of Pie

A MEERA PATEL MYSTERY

LEENA CLOVER

Leena Clover

Chapter 1

The gentle waves of the lake lapped against the shore. I huffed and puffed, trying to catch my breath.

"Maybe this wasn't a good idea," I complained.

Becky turned around and jogged back to me. She made it look so easy.

"Come on, Meera! We've hardly come two hundred meters."

She jogged in place, annoying me with the hint of laughter in her voice.

"I'm not fit for this," I let out, and sprawled on the tiny jogging path.

"Which is why you need to do this," Becky taunted me with a matter of fact voice.

The mid November morning was cool with temperatures in the mid 50s. My friend Becky had dragged me out to Lake Willow Springs and the 3 mile walking cum jogging track that went around it.

"The fresh air will do you good," Motee Ba, my grandma, had nodded eagerly.

Her eyes had met Becky's and a silent message passed through them. I was in a sort of funk, feeling sorry for myself, and people were plotting to get me out of it. I love these people, don't get me wrong, but I was in a weird frame of mind.

My name is Meera Patel, and I'm a 20 something grad school dropout who shelves books for a living. I live in a small college town in central Oklahoma. My dad Anand Patel is the head of the electrical engineering department at Pioneer Polytechnic, the local university. I put in some time at the local diner because I love to feed people and experiment with recipes. I live in a big ranch style house on the outskirts of town with my brother and

5

my grandparents. I met Becky in third grade and we've been inseparable ever since.

"Meera! You need to get fit!" Becky protested, trying to lift me off the ground.

The concrete path was cold and I could feel the chill through my thick sweats. My cheeks felt pink and my nose was cold.

"Do I have to?" I grumbled. "We stay on our feet long enough at the diner."

"That's different," Becky shook her head. "You need to get your heart rate up. Stop cribbing and look around. It's such a beautiful morning."

She gave me one last look and started running away.

"Wait," I called out, extending a hand. "At least help me get up."

Becky laughed and ran on.

I scrambled on to my fours, feeling my knees scrape against the rough path. I puffed again as I pulled myself up. My chest heaved with the effort and I decided to walk rather than jog. Some exercise was better than nothing, right? I promised myself my special French toast for breakfast. That put a spring in my step.

I trudged around the corner, trying to spot Becky in the distance. I took deep breaths, enjoying the misty morning, letting myself relax. I told myself I needed to get in shape. Then I spotted a welcome sight. A park bench!

It was a classic bench, painted green, set on a patch of grass a few feet off the walking track. It looked out on the water and another bench that graced the walking track on the opposite shore of the lake.

I collapsed on the bench and leaned back, taking in the area with my eyes half closed. It was a better way to enjoy the scenery, surely. Someone else had the same thoughts as me. A guy was lounging on the other corner of the bench, a hat pulled low over his eyes.

"What's up?" I said politely and closed my eyes.

Becky would be back any second to pull me off the bench.

A couple of minutes passed. I opened my eyes and glanced sideways. The guy was too well dressed to be homeless. A red and blue plaid shirt was tucked into well pressed khakis. A wedge of berry pie peeped out of his jacket. Crumbs of pie crust littered the bench and the ground by his feet.

He still hadn't returned my greeting. But I didn't take it to heart. The dead don't talk back, after all.

Some unknown reserve of energy I didn't know I had propelled me up.

"Becky," I roared, and ran flat out toward her.

A man dressed in nylon shorts and a half shirt ran toward me from the opposite direction. I waved him down.

"Something wrong?" he asked, not happy about having to break stride.

I pointed to the bench and poured out everything. Actually, I just blabbered gibberish. A bunch of drool rolled out of the side of my mouth and I wiped it away. The man jogged back to the bench and jabbed the man in the shoulder, something I hadn't dared to do.

The jogger looked at me and his eyes confirmed my suspicion. He pulled a cell phone out of his pocket and dialed 911. Becky had finally turned around and was coming toward me. Her mock anger changed to concern the moment she saw the look on my face.

"What's the matter, Meera?"

My finger shook as I pointed toward the bench. Flashing red and blue lights filled the park and three police cars converged on the road that led to the walking track.

A familiar stocky figure ambled down, looking important.

"Did you call the cops, Meera?" he demanded as soon as he saw me.

"No, I did," the other runner explained.

There wasn't much to say. The cops took in the scene and cordoned off the area.

"Is he …?" I asked slowly.

Stan looked me over and nodded.

"He's gone, Meera. It's been a while. What are you doing here anyway?"

I told him about our morning sojourn.

"Nothing wrong with trying to get fit," Stan Miller said. "I run five miles a day and do weights. I circle the lake on the weekends. But it's too much for me on a work day."

I mentally curled my fists. I really needed to shape up if Stan Miller was daring to give me fitness advice.

Becky was still in shock, and I hadn't heard a word out of her.

"You ready to go home?" I asked gently.

She barely nodded, staring in fascination at the man on the bench.

"Can we go now, Stan?" I asked, not sure of the response.

Stan gave a curt nod. "I know where to find y'all."

The truce with Stan Miller hadn't come easy. He had put me through the wringer the last few months. I had been the top suspect in the murder of Stan's girlfriend. Although his allegations didn't hold water, it had prompted me to do some leg work and actually prove myself innocent. Stan had apologized for his boorish behavior, and we had called a truce.

The truce was still in place, judging by his current conduct, but I had a feeling it was about to expire soon.

I turned the key of my Camry, uttering a silent prayer. The car started after a couple of tries and I heaved a sigh of relief. I didn't fancy asking Stan Miller for a ride.

Becky was quiet as I eased out of Willow Springs Lake Park onto Willow Drive. I swung a right onto Cedar and stopped at a traffic light.

"What are you thinking?" I asked Becky.

"I know that man," she said quietly.

"What?" I cried, as the light turned green and I took my foot off the brake. "Why didn't you say so?"

"I don't exactly know him, know him," she corrected herself. "I've seen him before."

I caught a green light at the highway intersection and turned right, speeding past Sylvie's Café & Diner and my pal Tony's gas station. I took a left onto Goat Farm Lane.

"Where?" I asked, slowing down.

The only houses on this road were ours and the Miller farm next door, which belonged to Stan Miller's uncle.

"Last night, at Sylvie's."

Becky works at Sylvie's Café. She is their full time cook and is good at it. I help out for a few hours every day, experimenting with recipes, adding some bold items to their menu.

"So what?" I asked. "Last night was quite busy, being a Sunday and all. Some 250-300 people must have come to the café."

Becky nodded. "I worked extra."

"What made you remember this guy then?" I asked.

"He was there with his girl friend. Sorry, fiancée. They were celebrating their recent engagement."

I pulled into our driveway and parked close to the house. We got out and trooped in through the back door.

It was barely 7 AM and my grandmother was boiling water for tea.

"Your Pappa's chai is almost done," she told me, her voice still groggy from sleep.

My grandfather is a stickler for his Masala Chai. Motee Ba wakes him every morning with a cup of his 'bed tea' and two digestive biscuits.

"I made a pot for you," Motee Ba signaled to the dripping coffee.

I thanked her and poured the steaming coffee into two large mugs. I dunked sugar and half & half into our mugs and handed one to Becky.

"Drink up," I ordered.

She took a few rapid sips and her color improved.

I was beating eggs in a bowl, adding in paprika. I dunked some thick Texas bread into the egg mixture and pulled out a container of salsa from the fridge. I had made it the previous evening.

Soon, I set two loaded plates on the kitchen island and urged Becky to eat.

"So he came to Sylvie's. So what?" I finally voiced the unspoken question.

"Did you see the pie, Meera?" Becky whispered.

I raised my eyebrows.

"That pie came from the diner. I know, because he ordered extra. That's why I remember him. They had a huge dinner, ordered pie a la mode, and then he ordered half a pie to take home with him. For the road, he said."

"We don't know what happened, Becky," I consoled her.

"I know, but I have this feeling ..."

"Hey, when do you want to talk about the Thanksgiving menu?" I tried to distract her.

Becky's feeling turned out to be much more than that.

Chapter 2

I showered and got ready for work. The day passed quickly. The student body was busy with final projects and assignments. The library was packed with kids trying to cram a semester's worth of knowledge, watch class videos, and discuss coursework with their class mates.

I drove to Sylvie's, eager to hear if there was any more news about the man. A spanking new building slightly opposite Sylvie's caught my eye. The fresh yellow paint almost seemed like an eye sore to me. To most other people in the town, it was fresh and cheerful. A large neon sign with 'Nancy's' in cursive hung in front of it. It was pink when lit up. A smaller sign proclaiming 'the fancy diner' hung below it, in case anyone had a doubt about the purpose of the building.

I shook my head and pulled up in front of Sylvie's. Swan Creek may be a small town, but we are loyal to our own. I didn't see any newcomer making it big with a diner, especially not in that spot.

Sylvie welcomed me with her signature hug as I breezed through the door. Her husband Jon called out to me from the kitchen and waved a spatula at me.

"Gumbo almost done," he called.

Sylvie and Jon Davis are as much a part of my family as Motee Ba or my Dad. They were the village that raised us motherless kids. Becky came out, trying to hide a frown.

"Meera, child, how are you?" Sylvie asked lovingly, trying to hide the concern in her voice. "Becky told me about earlier."

Jon came out and placed two plates of gumbo on a table. He motioned to Becky to take a break. I collapsed in a red vinyl booth and stirred my spoon through the gumbo, mixing a little rice in it. I looked out and Nancy's sat smack dab in the line of my vision.

"I suppose we have to get used to it," I groaned.

"They're a business, Meera," Sylvie reasoned. "Just like us. Can't stop anyone from earning an honest buck."

"I would like to see them do that," Becky hissed, swallowing a big spoonful of the fiery gumbo.

"None of our regulars are going there any time soon, Sylvie," I said loyally.

Honestly, I wasn't too sure.

The grapevine had been buzzing with all kinds of tidbits. Some said they had snow white table cloths on each table. Others said they had fresh flowers. French food was talked about, and artisan bread. We were all a bit nervous about the impact it would have on Sylvie's but no one wanted to voice their fears.

The small TV set over the counter was on and the news had come on. I saw a view of our local lake and some police tape.

"Turn that up, please," I urged Sylvie.

We listened agog as the announcer talked about the man who had been found on the bench by the lake.

"Police are looking into the cause of death of young Jordan Harris," the news anchor said.

"The 27 year old was in Swan Creek to celebrate his engagement with a Pioneer Poly student. Police have been tight lipped but our reporter couldn't help but notice the pie crumbs that littered the park bench where he was found. We all know there's only one place in Swan Creek that people go to for their pie fix. Does the pie figure in the cause of death of young Harris? Stay tuned for our updates…"

Sylvie turned the TV down, looking worried. The unspoken question was topmost in our minds.

"Becky says he was here yesterday," I spoke up. "Do you remember him too?"

Sylvie nodded.

"Jordan's been coming here for years. They made a cute couple. I gave them the best table. He was with that blue eyed blonde girl that comes around here often."

"Jessica," Becky supplied.

"Yes, her!" Sylvie nodded. "The one that talks a lot. Always has a word for Jon or me."

The Davises saw a wide variety of people at the diner. Some were barely civil to them, just tossing money their way for a meal. Some were polite but distant. Very few people actually took the time to show genuine interest in the people there.

Sylvie turned to Becky.

"Are you sure it was our pie? Couldn't it have been something else from the super market maybe?"

Becky's gaze said it all.

"I wrapped it myself, I remember. And I saw our logo on it. Tell her, Meera."

I backed Becky up.

"There's no doubt, Sylvie. I saw it too. But I don't see what the problem is."

"You know them cops," Jon said, coming out of the kitchen. "They tend to pick at the most obvious. What if they say our pie killed that boy?"

"Oh Jon, why would anyone say that?" I laughed.

The other three faces remained serious.

"We'll know soon enough," I muttered.

Becky tipped her head out of the window. There were lights inside Nancy's and a battered old wagon had drawn up. A couple of women got out. One of them was older, wearing a navy polka dot dress that stopped just above her knees. Her chin length bob was slightly retro. She was wearing sturdy shoes and stockings.

The other woman looked thirtyish and frumpy next to the older one. They turned around and looked at Sylvie's, and caught us standing together, staring at them.

Sylvie waved and smiled, motioning them to come meet us. Five minutes later, the two women were inside Sylvie's.

"Hello, I'm Nancy," the older woman said, offering her hand. "Nancy Robinson. And this is my girl Nellie."

We shook hands all around and Sylvie offered them coffee and pie.

"Thank you for your kindness, but we have a lot to do before tomorrow," Nancy declined politely.

"Tomorrow's our opening day," Nellie supplied.

"All the best to you," Sylvie said sincerely.

"Thanks a lot, dear," Nancy Robinson gushed. "I hope you're not worried about business?"

Sylvie just smiled and Jon grunted from inside.

"There's not much common between us, really. We serve a different clientele. The slightly posh one, you know."

I was working up to say something really nasty to the woman. I wasn't getting good vibes from her.

"My Nellie's gone to culinary school," Nancy went on. "She's a trained professional."

"Oh?" Sylvie said kindly. "We're looking forward to sampling your menu then."

Nancy took our leave and turned around. Nellie leaned forward and whispered in Sylvie's ear.

"Was that your pie they found on that park bench?"

Nancy shushed her daughter.

"What did I tell you Nellie? We don't want to smear anyone's name. The police haven't released any details yet."

The duo waved at us and walked out.

"What the …" I fumed the moment the door closed. "What were they trying to say anyway?"

Sylvie was trembling and Becky's cheeks had turned red.

"This is what I'm afraid of, child," Sylvie explained. "We saw enough of this earlier when that Miller boy hounded you about that missing girl."

"Let's hope he's a bit smarter now, Sylvie," I tried to calm everyone down.

"Imagine the nerve of that woman," Becky finally spit out. "She's already starting to spread nastiness. I bet that's exactly what their marketing plan is – smearing our name."

"Girls, girls," Sylvie called out, "don't get aggravated for no reason. How about that dinner prep?"

The diner got busy with the dinner rush and I fried batches of my special fried chicken. Becky finally calmed down as she assembled yet another Blue Plate Special with chicken kabobs on a skewer. It was a curry inspired recipe I had come up with and it had become very popular at the diner.

"When's Tony coming back?" Becky asked.

"Later tonight," I told her as I squirted some creamy yogurt and mint sauce over the kabobs.

Tony Sinclair is the third point that props up the triangle of our friendship. I had a big crush on Tony in high school, but being the jock he was, he deviated to the cheerleader types. Then we went off to college and did our thing. Our lives hadn't quite turned out as planned, and now we were both back home. Tony was mourning his ex and we had decided to be just friends for now.

After a couple of hours, I was beat. I said my goodbyes and

drove home, hoping Tony would get home soon. The day had been a bit drab without him.

Motee Ba, literally 'Big Ma', was at the stove making dinner.

Motee Ba just crossed 70. Together with Pappa, my 83 year old grandpa, she is the backbone of our family. My grandparents raised my brother Jeet and I after our mother went away several years ago. I don't know what I would do without her.

"How was your day, Meera?" she asked. "Dinner in thirty minutes."

I showered and trudged into the kitchen, looking for something to munch on.

Motee Ba pointed to a platter of *samosas* on the table.

"I made these earlier for Jeet and his friends. Just a few left for you."

I grabbed the tiny *samosa* dumpling and savored the flaky pastry cover. The potatoes and peas filling was mildly spiced and I gobbled a couple rapidly.

"Did you watch the news?" I asked my grandmother.

She nodded, looking worried.

"I don't know what this means for Sylvie and Jon."

"Relax, will you?" I burst out. "I said the same thing to Sylvie. Why make trouble where there isn't any?"

"It's early yet," Motee Ba refused to back out.

The clock struck nine and Motee Ba gave me the signal. I struck the dinner gong, letting everyone know it was time for dinner. My grandparents lived in British East Africa for several years and they have some habits that are a remnant of the Raj. The dinner gong is just one of them.

My brother Jeet tumbled in and dragged out a chair noisily.

"I'm starving!" he exclaimed and made a face when I mimicked his words as he said them.

At 19, he is always starving.

A tap tap sound came closer and my grandpa hobbled in, trying to walk fast with his cane. He slumped into a chair and looked around.

"Andy!" Pappa roared, calling out to his son, my father.

My dad is always last to the table, engrossed as he is in his books and papers.

"Why don't you get started?" Motee Ba motioned to Jeet, lifting the lid off a lentil stew and stir fried green beans.

Dinner commenced noisily, and my father finally joined the milieu. We leaned back one by one, sated after a simple Gujarati dinner.

"I hear you had quite a day today," Dad looked at me.

Motee Ba had brought him up to speed, apparently.

The enormity of my experience hadn't really sunk in yet. I shrugged.

"No tomfoolery this time, girl," Pappa boomed, tapping his cane. "I'm warning you."

"Pappa," I protested. "What do you mean?"

"You know what, Meera," my Dad said calmly.

"I had no choice," I protested, referring to the time earlier in the semester when I'd had to defend myself.

"Sylvie may be in trouble," Motee Ba told everyone. "We don't know for sure yet, but you all know how harmful rumors can be."

Dad gave Motee Ba a questioning glance. I told him about the pie crumbs found at the scene.

"I think you're jumping ahead, both of you," Dad said, picking up his plate and putting it in the sink.

Jeet started rinsing the plates and loading the dishwasher.

"Say someone tries to implicate Sylvie," Motee Ba mused. "We won't just look the other way, will we?"

Pappa was silent, and Dad walked out, back to his study. I answered the question they didn't want to.

"Of course we won't, Motee Ba."

Chapter 3

I woke early the next morning and chomped through a bowl of cereal, eager to get to work. Becky hadn't turned up for our morning run and I was glad. I turned into Tony's gas station, hoping to meet him.

I leaned against the heavy glass door, and whiffed at the familiar scent of Zest soap in the air. Tony grinned at me from behind the counter, looking fresh out of the shower, his wet hair curling around his ear.

"Hey Meera!" he called out.

"Have you heard?" I asked, unable to hold back any more.

He looked up as he rang up my large mug of the special holiday blend. His eyes were full of concern.

"That must've been quite a shock!"

I had dreamed about the dead guy. I was finally beginning to get creeped out as the shock wore off.

"I actually talked to him, you know," I exclaimed. "I said, 'wasup', and I was waiting for an answer."

Tony came out from behind the counter and wrapped his arms around me. I let myself be hugged properly.

"Nice day you chose to be out of town."

We walked out to my car and stood side by side, leaning against it. I sipped the hot coffee, trying to draw some much needed energy from it.

"How are Jon and Sylvie taking it?" Tony asked.

"They're worried. What if ..."

"Try to relax, Meera. We don't know enough to worry."

"But we know Stan," I told Tony.

"Let's hope he's a bit smarter now," Tony sighed.

The day passed in a blur and I was rushed off my feet. I was putting in extra hours to make up for the Thanksgiving break.

I was bone tired by the time I drove up to Sylvie's. There was a lot of activity at Nancy's. Colorful red and white balloons fluttered in the evening breeze. White fairy lights were strung across the building. The parking lot was packed and some more cars lined the curb.

I parked my car in Sylvie's lot and stood looking at what was happening. Becky came out of the diner.

"They had a big to do this afternoon. It's their opening day."

"Looks festive," I commented and went inside with Becky.

The kitchen was prepped for the dinner rush. A few pies were cooling on the counter. A half cut pecan pie lay under a glass dome.

"You girls hungry?" Sylvie asked as Becky came out with two trays.

"Grilled cheese with three slices, just the way you like it."

She placed the two trays loaded with a sandwich and bowls of tomato soup. We made quick work of the food.

"When are we talking about the Thanksgiving menus?" I asked, looking up at Sylvie and Becky.

"How 'bout tomorrow?" Sylvie asked. "You look done in today, child."

I nodded and went in as a large group of locals entered. Earlier this summer, Becky and I had convinced Jon and Sylvie to modernize their menu a bit. The diner was now becoming well known for the veggie burgers and *pakoras*, my Indian spiced fried chicken and gourmet sandwiches.

"Black bean burgers today?" I asked Becky, referring to the daily specials and she nodded.

I shaped the patties and placed them gently on the grill. I placed slices of pepperjack cheese on top of each. We served them with a chipotle sour cream and sliced avocadoes with seasoned fries. It wasn't for the faint of heart. But we love our chili over here in the South, and the burger was becoming popular once people got over the idea of going meatless.

An hour passed in a blur. Then there was a buzz outside. I looked at Becky in alarm and we rushed out. My heart sank as I spied the now familiar flashing lights of a cop car in the parking lot.

The door opened and Stan Miller walked in, flanked by two more policemen. Becky and I stood on either side of Sylvie, ready to support her if necessary.

"Jon Davis?" Stan asked.

"You know who I am, young man," Jon snorted. "Get on with it."

"We are investigating the death of Jordan Harris. You need to come with us."

My eyes widened as I put my hands on my hips.

"Wait a minute, Stan," I spit out. "What do you mean, go with you? Why?"

"I'm just doing my job, Meera," Stan looked at me reproachfully. "I need to take their statements."

"Then why didn't you just call and ask them to come over? Why all this drama?"

Stan turned red.

"We wanted to catch them before they fled."

"And where are they going to flee?" I asked gently. "Stan, these people have been living in Swan Creek since before you and I were born. This diner is their livelihood. They're not going anywhere. Why would you think so, anyway?"

"Well, there's some talk of a tainted pie …" Stan began.

"Do you have proof?" I demanded.

"It's too early for any of that, Meera," Stan admitted.

Sylvie had come out and was calmly listening to our exchange.

"We'll come over right now and give your statement. But we are coming there on our own."

Stan nodded and stepped outside reluctantly.

I called Motee Ba and Tony and brought them up to speed. Becky was asked to keep the diner going.

I was about to usher Jon and Sylvie into my car when Tony's pickup screeched to a stop. He gently helped the couple into the back seat of his cab. I rode shotgun and we headed to the local police station.

I don't know how but Motee Ba had managed to beat us there.

Stan ushered Jon and Sylvie into an empty room. He held up his hand as I was about to follow.

"Just them at this time," he warned.

I paced the lobby with Tony. Motee Ba sat still in a hard plastic chair, her back ramrod straight. I admired her tight control.

"Sit down, Meera," she ordered after I had paced the short space for the hundredth time.

After what seemed like hours but was barely forty minutes, the door opened and Sylvie and Jon came out, ushered by Stan.

"Thanks for this," Stan told them.

"We have nothing to hide," Jon said simply.

Without a word, we filed out and headed back to the diner. Becky rushed out when she saw us, and sighed in relief as she saw Sylvie get out of the car.

"How about something to drink?" she asked, and I nodded.

We soon had a hot drink in front of us. Sylvie recounted what had happened.

"That boy just stopped breathing. They think it could be some kind of reaction to what he ate."

"You mean poison?" I burst out.

Jon shrugged.

"They are not actually saying anything, because they don't know for sure themselves."

"Is it the food, or isn't it?" Motee Ba asked impatiently.

She was beginning to lose her cool.

"They just don't know," Sylvie said in a tired voice. "But they do know the boy ate dinner here. Many people saw him. And we are not denying that."

"Wait a minute, though," I interrupted as I thought of something.

"Didn't that girl eat the same thing? And hundreds of people who came to the diner that day."

Jon nodded along.

"That's what I told them. But then they found that pie. Looks like it's the last thing he ate."

"Someone called in a tip about tainted pie," Sylvie sobbed. "Imagine, my pie causing harm to someone."

"But that's a load of crap," Becky burst out. "Who would do that? And if there was something wrong with the pie, why aren't more people turning up sick?"

"Maybe they fell sick and just haven't told us yet?" Tony ventured and Becky and I both smacked him on the head.

"We're talking something more serious than a headache," Motee Ba reasoned. "I don't see anyone in this town doing this kind of thing. Calling in to the police, making mad allegations? Why, that's just plain devious. Who would do that?"

My eyes met Becky's and we both pointed out of the window. Dance music blared out of speakers mounted outside. Nancy's was lit up like a Christmas tree. Nancy Walker had hinted at a tainted pie.

"They would!" I pointed a finger out of the window.

No one said anything for a minute.

Then I narrated what had happened the earlier day when the mother-daughter duo had come in to say Hi.

"That's just bad karma," Motee Ba said bitterly. "I wouldn't start a new venture by lying about the competition."

Tony stood up and walked up to the counter. He cut a wedge of pecan pie and slid it onto a plate. He came back to the table and forked a piece into his mouth.

"That's what I think of tainted pie," he said.

Jon slapped him on the back, and Sylvie pinched his cheek.

"We sell the most amount of pies around this time, what with Thanksgiving and all," Sylvie said. "I've got advanced orders for dozens of them pies."

"I checked the order book earlier today," Becky confirmed. "Most people will be coming to pick up their order the day before Thanksgiving. The ones who are traveling will get theirs a day or two early. And then the late orders are willing to pick up their pie as late as Thursday afternoon, just before dinner."

"That's less than a week to fill all those orders, Sylvie," Motee Ba reminded her. "I will be pitching in as usual. Let's forget all this nonsense and draw up a plan for how to cook all these pies."

Sylvie smiled.

"We plan to be open for the holiday this year. Many of our regulars have requested a Thanksgiving meal. It's going to be reservations only. We'll serve at 2 PM and close at 4. That still gives us time for our own dinner."

Tony's parents were hosting all of us for Thanksgiving this year and I was looking forward to it.

"Stan seemed slightly more reasonable today, didn't he?" I admitted grudgingly.

"But he does get carried away. Why did he have to come here with all those lights flashing?" Motee Ba complained.

We said our goodbyes as Jon and Sylvie closed up for the day. I followed Motee Ba's car as we slowly drove home.

"Things don't look good, Meera," Motee Ba said quietly as she brushed my hair later that night, tying it into two plaits.

This was a nightly ritual when I was growing up, and Motee Ba still does it any time she or I are disturbed. It's our way of letting off steam.

"Sylvie and Jon have always stood by us," I was serious as I thought of what lay ahead. "I'm going to do my best to see them through this."

Chapter 4

The next few days were busy. Becky insisted we stick to our plans and still go on that morning run.

"Think of all the extra calories we're going to consume for Thanksgiving," she warned. "You won't fit into your swim wear in the spring. And we just have to do something different this year for Spring Break. You promised!"

"That's in March!" I cried. "Why do I have to work on it now?"

Becky relented only about one thing. Instead of Willow Springs Lake Park, we went to the track at Pioneer Poly. I just couldn't bear the thought of running through that park again, wondering what lay around the corner.

The extra hours at work were hell on my feet. I was glad my sneakers went with my usual garb of jeans and long sleeved tees. In the evening, I helped Sylvie with shopping and prepping for all her pie orders and worked on a couple of new recipes for the big Thanksgiving dinner.

"Try this," I said, sticking a sauce laden spatula in front of Becky. "This is my second batch."

Becky licked the spoon and frowned for a second. Then her face broke out in a smile as she fanned her tongue.

"That's awesome. Sweet at first but then the warmth of the spices seeps through. What is it?"

"Just my spiced cranberry relish. Do you think it's good enough for the day?"

"People are gonna love it," Becky enthused. "It's sweet, tart and spicy. Different!"

I grinned with pleasure, and turned as the phone rang.

Sylvie beat me to it. She spoke for a couple of minutes and then hung up. She picked up the order book lying on the counter and wrote something in it. Mostly, she just struck out a few lines.

"Sylvie?" I raised my eyebrows, trying to stay calm.

She shook her head, looking beat.

"More cancellations. At this rate, we won't be needing too many pies this year."

"What about our regulars?" I asked. "Jon's and Pappa's friends, and the ladies in your Bingo group."

"They haven't called yet, but they will."

I tried to console Sylvie. There had been no official statement yet about the cause of death in our local crime, but the jungle patrol was in full swing. People were calling in to cancel their pie orders. A few pies wouldn't make a difference to the diner business, but it was the loss of reputation that worried Jon and Sylvie.

Tony turned up at the library the next day. We have a standing lunch date at least 2-3 times a week.

"Where do you want to eat?" he asked.

"Let's just go to the food court. The sooner I get back, the sooner I can get out of here."

We walked to the food court and I got my usual chicken sandwich. Tony had a double cheeseburger. We both got fries. I was working out, after all.

In between bites of the crispy chicken and greasy fries, I brought Tony up to speed.

"What can we do to help?" he asked, cutting to the chase.

A group of women sat down at a table next to us. They were vaguely familiar. Swan Creek is a small town. I know the handful of locals, and people I went to school with. And then there are people who work on campus. I remembered these women from the bursar's office.

"My Tommy's raising a stink," one plump woman complained to the other, dousing her salad in a creamy dressing.

"Why?" the other woman asked, shoveling a big bite of salad in her mouth.

All three women were in their fifties, wearing plain skirts and blouses, with a string of pearls at their throat and gray hair at the temples. They were slightly overweight, and all three were eating salads drenched in some creamy dressing.

"He says my pie crust is not flaky enough. And it never gets cooked. His Mama doesn't like it."

"Aren't you getting your usual order?" the third woman asked.

The other two looked at her as if she was from another planet.

"Don't be a fool, Ada! Don't you know?"

Ada continued to be clueless.

"Know what?"

An urgent whispering ensued and Ada sat back, her eyes gleaming. She was slightly out of breath.

"I had no idea," she swore.

"I cancelled our order last night. And you should do it too."

"But do we know for sure?" Ada dared to contradict them.

"Who cares?" the first woman pounced. "Are you willing to risk your life for the sake of that pie?"

Ada shook her head.

"There's got to be some truth in it," the second woman said. "No smoke without fire."

I tapped my foot in anguish as I ploughed through my sandwich, listening to this crap. Tony kept a firm hold on my hand, keeping me from getting up and giving them a piece of my mind.

"Nothing you say's going to change their minds," he stated.

Tony's ears had turned red, a sure sign he was angry. He just had a better control over his actions than I did.

"What I don't get is, where is this coming from?" I fumed.

"I saw the news last night. They were showing that segment again. They mentioned that some pie was found on the bench."

"So what? Who told them it came from Sylvie's?"

Tony shrugged.

"Chances are it did! Everyone in Swan Creek knows Sylvie's."

"I think it's those two women – Nancy and Nellie. They're the ones behind this."

"Calm down, Meera. You don't know that. And you're doing the same thing, accusing them of something without proof."

I was getting tired of the whole thing.

We walked back to the library and Tony waved goodbye. I dragged myself to the Camry and pulled in at Sylvie's, an hour later than usual. It was past 6 PM, and normally, I would've had to park at the back. The parking lot at Sylvie's was almost deserted. Cars lined the opposite end of the street.

I pushed the door open with a heavy heart and my eyes met Sylvie's as she stood staunchly behind the counter. A berry pie was cooling on the counter.

"How are you, dear?" Sylvie tried to be upbeat.

Becky came out of the kitchen.

"Is there some event at Pioneer tonight? Our dinner crowd hasn't come in yet."

I shook my head. The order book lay open on a table, and several rows in it were scratched out.

"The phone's been ringing off the hook," Sylvie told me just as it trilled again.

"Sylvie's Diner," Becky answered.

Her face changed and became mutinous.

"Any reason?" she asked. "Change of plans? Well, you better finalize your plans next time before making reservations. We'll be charging a fine for cancellations."

She slammed the phone down. Without a single word, she grabbed the pen on the counter and scratched through another row in the order book. She almost tore through the paper.

A lone tear appeared in Sylvie's eye.

"Calm down, child. It's just a rough patch. All a part of life."

"How many people coming for dinner now?" I asked.

Sylvie looked at the book.

"Seven."

"Less work for us," I tried to joke.

"I think I'm going to cancel the dinner. Make it easier on the remaining people."

Sylvie was thoughtful. Jon had come out, untying his apron. He hung it on a hook and placed an arm around Sylvie.

"That seems best for now, Cherie. We'll do it next year."

I thought of the elaborate menu we had come up with, the recipes we had tested.

"Meera tried out all them recipes," Sylvie groaned.

"Don't worry about me," I told her. "I can make some of my cranberry relish at Aunt Reema's."

I stopped at Tony's on the way home, hoping he was still working. He came out when he saw me pull up.

"What's up, Meera. Any news?"

I poured out everything in a rush and paced the parking lot.

Tony pulled me closer and we sat on the hood of my car, oblivious to the icy wind blowing in.

"How about a dinner date?" he asked.

"Are you out of your mind?" I rolled my eyes.

Tony sometimes makes these lame attempts at humor to diffuse a stressful situation.

"I hear there's this fancy new place in town. Why don't we check it out?"

I stared at Tony, thinking he had completely lost it. Then I connected the dots.

"Would this place be called Nancy's?" I asked, putting on an impish smile.

"It might," he grinned.

"Thank you, kind sir! I would love to accept your kind invitation."

I fluttered my eyelids and fanned myself and we burst out laughing. I went home in a better mood. Dinner was almost served and Motee Ba had sounded the gong.

"I'm sorry I haven't been much help around here," I apologized to her. "It's all these extra hours at work. Next week should be better."

"At least I get to eat my wife's cooking," Pappa said happily as he came in.

"Live it up, Pappa. It's back to my one pot meals next week."

Motee Ba and I shared a smile as Pappa muttered something.

The next day flew by and I drove home to get dressed for my date. I had told Sylvie I had some work related crisis. We didn't want to tell anyone about our plans. At least not until they yielded something concrete.

I put on a frock in honor of the date. It was a burnt orange silk with simple lines. I pulled on brown boots and borrowed a pair of Motee Ba's garnet earrings. I spritzed on some Shalimar perfume and I was ready.

I heard a car pull up and I ran to the door.

"Let him come in," Motee Ba twinkled. "Make him wait a few minutes."

"It's not a real date, Motee Ba!" I burst out.

"You are sharing a meal with a handsome young man. Someone you like. Whatever your reason for going out, it's a date."

I kissed my granny and we shared a smile. The doorbell rang. Tony had chosen to enter by the front door, so maybe there was something to this dating business.

"For you, Meera," my brother Jeet yelled, pitching his voice louder than the blaring TV.

I went out with my granny.

Tony hugged and kissed her.

"Hello Granny. Don't I look good?"

He twirled and made a big show of it. Motee Ba pinched his cheek.

"Mom told me to ring the doorbell," Tony whispered in Motee Ba's ear.

Tony was wearing khakis and a snow white shirt. His sports coat made him look grown up and handsome.

"Shall we?" he asked me, extending an arm.

I held on to his arm tightly and we waved goodbye to the company assembled in the living room. Pappa tapped his cane, annoyed at the interruption. Dad was closeted in his study, as usual.

The November sky was already dark, even though it was barely 6 PM. Orange and purple streaks hugged the horizon and the clear skies promised a starry night.

We were both quiet as Tony merged onto the highway. He had brought his mother's sedan for the occasion. It was easier to get into than the pickup. This kind of thoughtfulness is typical of Tony. Plus the car made me feel special.

It took all of five minutes to reach Nancy's, and before I could pick out a CD I wanted to listen to, Tony was trying to squeeze into a parking space in the crowded parking lot.

He rushed out to open the door for me. I beamed at him and took his hand as he helped me out. We wouldn't have to pretend much to look like a couple on a date.

"There's a 30 minute wait," the hostess, a young chit who looked barely sixteen informed us saucily.

"I have a reservation. Sinclair."

Tony smiled at the girl and she blushed.

"Right this way, Sir," she almost bowed, ushering us in.

I didn't have to wonder why Nancy's was the fancy diner.

Chapter 5

Round tables filled the cavernous space and booths lined the tall glass windows. Unlike the vinyl booths at Sylvie's, these were made of real leather. The tables were of mixed sizes, some cozy enough for two. Snowy white tablecloths sparkled, and a votive candle in small hurricane glasses graced each table. A small bud vase held a fresh rose.

"This is beautiful," I exclaimed.

I believe in giving credit where it is due. Someone had done a great decorating job for Nancy's. Not to mention the amount of money they must have sunk in it. It all seemed a bit much for our small town.

The hostess ushered us to a table in the center of the room. It was set for two, but it was spacious. A server turned up and took our drink orders.

They had wine, another feather in their crown.

The dinner special was Coq Au Vin, some kind of fancy French style chicken. Tony ordered steak with herbed butter.

"Boy, they really are fancy," Tony noted.

We gobbled our salads and took our time over the entrees. I was looking out for a glimpse of Nancy or Nellie.

My eyes strayed to an elderly woman who sat alone in a booth. She was reading a book and eating soup. She had her back to me but something about her seemed familiar. Maybe someone from campus, I thought.

Nellie came out, dressed in a chef's jacket.

"Welcome to Nancy's, the fancy diner," she said. "I hope y'all are enjoying your food?"

We nodded and complimented her. I waited for a sign of recognition but Nellie moved on to another table.

Our server returned with the dessert menu, right when we were finishing our entrees.

"How about some pie?" Tony asked. "Some apple pie a la mode sounds just the thing after that steak."

"We don't serve pies," the server said.

"Not a single one?" I asked incredulously.

He shook his head.

"But why?"

"We just don't. There was an incident recently in this town. It was pie related."

He hesitated as he said 'incident'.

"Are you talking about Jordan Harris?" I questioned. "There is no definite proof that any pie was involved."

"How can you get away without serving pie, anyway?" Tony asked.

We live in pie country. We want our chicken fried steak and our barbecued ribs, but they mean nothing without pie. Apple, berry, pecan, banana cream, lemon meringue – we want them all.

The server began to look worried.

"I have a six layer chocolate cake, and a caramel swirl cheesecake. Or carrot cake."

"Why no pie?" Tony persisted.

The server leaned forward.

"Look, it's company policy. We will not be serving pie, and if anyone asks for it, we are supposed to tell them about the pie related incident."

"So you just want to turn people off pie?" I demanded.

"Just doing my job," the server shrugged.

"Let's just get dessert across the street," Tony said loudly. "At Sylvie's."

"Are you sure you want to do that?" a woman at an adjoining table hissed.

"Of course I'm sure," Tony said confidently.

The woman was shaking her head, widening her eyes at her companion. A man who sat with her spoke up.

"I wouldn't take that kind of a risk, son. Not with such a pretty young lady by my side."

He leered at me and the woman rapped him on the knuckles.

Tony asked for the check. He motioned me to stay quiet. I was boiling inside but we had got what we came for. Now we knew why people were calling in to cancel orders and reservations.

The older woman in the booth paid up before us and walked by. I felt something familiar but couldn't place it.

We walked out and got in the car. Tony crossed the road and parked in Sylvie's empty parking lot.

"You look pretty, child," Sylvie smiled as we entered. "And so do you." She smiled at Tony.

Becky came out and her eyes popped out of her head.

"Were you two on a date?"

Tony looked embarrassed.

"Sort of," I admitted. "More a covert mission."

"We don't get them fancy words, Meera," Jon teased. "Spit it out clearly."

I gave them a quick account of where we'd had dinner. And then I told them about the dessert menu at Nancy's.

"See, I was right!" Becky exclaimed. "Those two witches ..."

"Becky," Sylvie warned. "We'll not be talking bad stuff about our neighbors."

"She's right though, isn't she?" I argued.

Sylvie seemed shocked. She sat down in a booth and Jon collapsed next to her.

"All these years we ran the business," Jon began. "We never pointed a finger at other restaurants."

"It's not just them, though," Tony summed up. "The locals are talking too."

"Yeah!" Becky pressed on. "So there's some really bad rumors going around. And we know who's spreading them. Now what?"

"It won't last, will it?" Sylvie's voice was hopeful. "People know us, right? They'll be back in a few days or weeks."

"But how long can we afford to take a hit, honey?" Jon asked. "All our Thanksgiving orders have been cancelled. We need to do something now!"

"We need help. Yes Sir!" Sylvie nodded. "If it was just a few less pie orders, it wasn't a big deal. But we've had almost no business for over a week. We can't stay afloat much longer if this continues."

They looked at each other, and then they looked at me.

"Will you help us, Meera?"

"Anything for you, Sylvie. But I'm not sure what I can do."

"We saw how you helped find that missing girl. And you already found out who's spreading nasty tales about my pie. Can you prove the pie had nothing to do with that poor boy's death?"

I looked at Tony and Becky, my staunch helpers.

"What do you say, guys?"

"We're with you!" Becky got excited and brandished her spatula, ready for battle.

"So you want me to find out who killed that man on the bench?" I spelled it out clearly, in case I had been mistaken.

Everyone in the room nodded.

"I can try."

I was amazed at the faith these people have in me.

Jon and Sylvie were all smiles.

"We knew we could count on you," Sylvie said, slipping behind the counter.

"Where do we start?" I asked Becky.

"How about that girl who was here with the guy? The girl friend?"

"I'm not sure I remember her," I told Becky.

"You will, once you see her. She comes around here often enough. Let's make a list of anything we can think of and we can talk about it tomorrow. I have to close up now."

I nodded as I stifled a yawn.

Tony drove me home.

"I had a good time," I said shyly. "Maybe we should do this again."

"Sure, anytime," Tony smiled, ruffling my hair, kissing me on the cheek.

He walked me to the kitchen door. Motee Ba was sipping herbal tea, waiting for us. We gave her the lowdown on what had happened. She bristled with anger when she heard about what Nancy Robinson was up to.

"You did good, kids!" she patted Tony on the back.

"What's Dad going to feel about this?" I asked.

Both Pappa and Dad had been against my trying to find Jyothi, the missing girl, earlier this year. But I had taken a stand and they had relented. At that time, my own neck was on the line. I wondered how they would feel about me taking on some amateur sleuthing for someone else. I knew they were worried about my safety. They thought it was too dangerous. Then Sylvie's kind face flashed in front of me. I tightened my resolve.

"He'll be against it," Motee Ba voiced my thoughts. "He will advise Jon to hire a lawyer."

"I have your back, Meera," Tony reassured me. "But aren't you losing sight of one thing? What about the rumors? Shouldn't someone confront that woman about this? I mean, she's causing harm without reason. It's defamation. It's against the law!"

Tony went to law school for a couple of semesters. He knows this stuff.

"Talking about it will only draw more attention. I think it's best to ignore those rumors. And deny them if anyone talks about it to us."

Motee Ba looked mutinous.

"Sylvie and I can talk to that woman. We'll put her out of business."

We talked about Thanksgiving dinner at Tony's for a while and then he bid us goodnight.

"You're taking a big step, Meera," Motee Ba said as she brushed my hair later that night. "I'm proud of you."

Chapter 6

I got out of bed with a sense of purpose the next morning. I rushed through my shower and entered the kitchen in a hurry. Motee Ba was standing over a skillet, flipping *theplas*. These unleavened flatbreads are like tortillas and they are a staple in our family.

I placed two *theplas* on a plate, slathered them with *chundo*, a type of mango chutney, and tore off a piece. I fanned my mouth as I tried to swallow the hot piece of bread. A car honked outside and someone rapped loudly on the door.

I had a sudden déjà vu moment, thinking about the time Stan Miller had come barging into our kitchen earlier in the summer. The door opened inwards and sure enough, Stan Miller sauntered in.

I stared at him like a deer caught in the headlights.

"Morning, Patels!" he called out cheerfully, and I sighed.

He came in peace, apparently.

"I have an update, Meera," he explained. "I thought it best to come report in person."

Motee Ba fixed a plate for Stan. She handed him a knife and fork and he made quick work of the thin, flaky theplas. Stan had grown up on the neighboring farm, and he had been in and out of our kitchen, just like Tony and Becky. He never misses a chance to enjoy anything Motee Ba cooks.

"Well?" I asked, gulping some coffee, waiting for Stan to spill the beans.

Pappa came in just then, tapping his cane. He settled down in his usual chair and smacked his lips at the aroma in the kitchen. Dad and Jeet would soon be coming in.

"Don't mind them," I waved around me. "Go on."

"It's about the woman," Stan began.

A woman had been observed loitering around campus since summer. The police thought she was following me around.

Motee Ba switched off the stove and came and sat next to me, ignoring Pappa's frown.

"She's been spotted in town again. She's driving a different car this time."

I sucked in a breath.

"Is she following any of us again?"

"Not to our knowledge," Stan told me.

"What does she do all day?" I asked curiously.

"Nothing specific, I think. Drives around, walks around the campus, walks around in Wal-Mart, eats in restaurants ... that's about it. Last I checked, none of that is a crime."

"Why are we worried about her then?" Motee Ba asked.

"She's a loose end," Stan explained. "A lot of things pointed to her last time, in Prue's case."

Stan reddened a bit when he mentioned Prudence, his ex. She had been found dead earlier in the summer. Her death had been linked to the disappearance of another student. I had been implicated in the case, and had been a suspect. Stan had sung a pretty different tune at the time.

"How can you be sure it's the same woman?" I asked.

"We're sort of sure. She matches the general description. Of course, we didn't have any photos then. We are going to try and get some this time. But like I said, she is not implicated in any crime. So we can't just tape her or follow her all the time."

"What do you want from me then?" I asked.

"I wanted to ask if you had noticed anyone following you again. Just keep an eye out and let us know immediately. We are prepared to take her in this time."

I promised Stan I would be circumspect.

"What about the guy on that park bench? Any more news about him?"

"I can't talk about that, Meera," Stan puffed up. "We're still working on it."

"Someone said his heart gave out," I volunteered.

"Well, that much is true," Stan admitted grudgingly. "But we don't know the cause yet. Could be caused by something he ate or drank. He was a healthy young man, you know."

"What about the pie they found on him? Do you think it had anything to do with it?"

Stan shook his head.

"Can't say. Hey, I love Sylvie's pies myself. I've been eating them for years. If the pie was tainted, it happened after the pie came out of that diner."

"I'm going to try and help Sylvie," I started, expecting Stan to strike me down.

"Be careful, Meera. You're smart. You helped us a lot in Prue's case. Personally, I will take any help I can get. This has us stumped."

He picked up his hat and stepped out of the door.

Pappa was tapping his cane impatiently.

"Hansa, where are my *theplas*? How long are you going to make me wait for them?"

He glared at me next.

"You stay out of trouble, girl! This family has had enough nonsense this year. You should be living with your husband, raising kids, not running around with this tomfoolery."

I escaped before Dad came in to add his two cents.

I met Tony and Becky at our favorite Thai restaurant for lunch. It was quieter than any place on campus.

"Have you made a list?" I asked, pulling out a piece of paper.

"We need to know where the guy was from," Becky plunged ahead. "All we know is he has a ranch or a farm somewhere down south. But exactly where? Who does he live with? Like, does he have a family?"

"I'll look that up," I promised, writing down the first item on my agenda.

"What about the girl friend?" Tony asked.

I punched him in the shoulder.

"Of course you would think about her!"

"Didn't you say her name was Jessica?" I asked Becky. "Got a last name?"

Becky didn't remember a last name. She thought the girl studied something related to food or chemistry. I added another item on my list. I could look up the current students in some of the departments.

"What about those nasty women?" Becky asked. "Why are they suddenly in Swan Creek? Where did they come from?"

"I want to know that too, Becky," I objected, "but how is that relevant to Jordan Harris?"

Becky's face fell.

"I'll write it down but let's keep it aside for now," I consoled her.

The waitress brought over our Red Curry and Pad Thai noodles. We gobbled the spicy food, sniffling and wiping the tears that rolled down our eyes. We washed it down with icy coconut water.

"That was great," Tony burped, finally pushing his plate away.

I told them about Stan's visit.

"So what is it you are supposed to do, Meera?" Becky asked.

I shrugged. "I never saw the woman. So I don't really believe in her."

I knew this would annoy Tony and he interrupted me as expected.

"That woman is real, Meera. I saw her follow us all the way to Wichita and back."

"Cool your jets, bubba!" I held up a hand. "Maybe you should be on the lookout for her, then," I said. "Since you're the only one who's at least had a glimpse of her."

"You can bet I will do that," Tony promised.

"I know there's no way there was anything wrong with the pie," I began. "But say we have to prove it. We should be prepared."

"What do you want to know?" Becky asked.

"Where does all the stuff for the pie come from?" I asked.

"It's all made in house," Becky said defensively. "The flour, butter, sugar is from our usual supplier. It's the same we use for making anything in the diner. The fruits are fresh from the market. The nuts are bought whole sale from our supplier."

"Was there anything different that day?" I asked.

Becky shook her head.

"You think I haven't gone over this in my mind? The pie we served was fresh, baked earlier that afternoon. Everything was as usual, using Sylvie's secret recipe. There was not a single ingredient that was different."

"What about any spice or any other flavoring?" I persisted. "You know, you like to experiment with the food."

"With the regular food yes, but not the pies," Becky denied. "The pies are all Sylvie. I don't touch them at all. And I wouldn't dare to add anything to them."

Tony looked at me.

"Is that good or bad?"

"At this point, hard to say. One might say there's something toxic in Sylvie's kitchen."

I held up my hand, cutting off both Tony and Becky's protests.

"I'm just saying."

We gathered our stuff and Tony dropped me off.

I was manning the front desk at the library the rest of the afternoon. I tried some searches within the school network, in between answering students' queries and keeping an eye on the audio-video room.

A search in the student directory threw up thirty three Jessicas. Boy, sure looks like a popular name, I thought.

I decided to weed out the doctoral students first. There was one girl called Jessica in Architecture and another in Chemical Engineering. Becky had mentioned something about food or nutrition. I checked the list of master's students. There was one in Management, another in English, one in Teacher's Ed and one in Agriculture. None of these seemed right.

I decided to check out the Agriculture department. I called the general department line and asked about the girl. I was hoping someone would be ready to gossip.

"Hello," I spoke in a hushed voice.

"I'm calling for Jessica. She left a ring here for resizing. Her order is ready."

"We don't take messages for students," a voice drawled at the other end.

"Oh? But this is the number she gave us. I'm sure she must be eager to wear her engagement ring."

"Look! I can see you are calling from somewhere on campus. So quit yanking my chain, alright? The Jessica I know is nowhere near getting engaged."

Strike One! I had managed to eliminate one of the Jessicas. I was pretty sure the one studying management or English wouldn't be studying food or nutrition. And the undergraduates were too young to be getting engaged. Weren't they?

On a hunch, I walked over to the Chemistry department. I preferred to tackle this in person.

A couple of women were working at their computers outside a door labeled Director, Chemical Engineering. Another door to the right listed the Head of Department and a smaller door a few paces to the left was for the Assistant Director of Admissions. This is pretty much a common set up for every department at Pioneer. A cluster of desks seated a bunch of secretaries and coordinators. They were all busy tapping on their keyboards, staring at their computer screens. One girl looked up and smiled as I entered.

"May I help you?" she asked.

"Er, I'm looking for Jessica," I dived in.

The girl's smile froze. She leaned forward and whispered.

"She's not in. She's in deep shock. We are not supposed to give out information about her."

"I was hoping to pay my respects. We went to school together. Then we lost touch. I came as soon as I heard."

I crossed my fingers behind my back, hoping my lie would fly.

The girl grinned naughtily.

"Jessica's not from around here. She's from some place down south on the Texas border. And I know you. You work at that diner."

"Busted," I admitted, holding up my hand in a peace sign.

"Look, I really do want to pay my respects."

"She's holed up at the Harris ranch," the girl said. "But don't tell anyone you heard it from me."

I thanked her and stopped at a vending machine. I treated myself to a giant cookie and a can of soda. All I had to do now was find out where the Harris family lived. I already knew they didn't live in Swan Creek.

A few dozen piles of books were waiting to be reshelved. I did that and hardly noticed when the clock crept past five. I stayed on to run another online search.

I loaded up a search engine program in my browser and looked for farms in Oklahoma. There were just too many. I entered the names for nearby counties one by one. Then I tried to find ranches. I typed in 'working ranch' to narrow down the search. I found one about sixty miles south east.

"It looks like a big thing," I told Becky and Tony at the diner later that evening.

The diner was deserted. Other than a couple of regulars, no one had come in for dinner. Sylvie and Jon were trying to be upbeat.

"How big?" Tony asked.

"Over five hundred acres. They have a big lake and cabins for rent. And they have horses."

Tony whistled.

"Who manages all that?"

"That's what we have to find out. Maybe we should just drive down there this weekend and talk to someone."

"I have a better idea," Tony winked. "Why don't we go there for the weekend? Just us kids though."

Becky's face fell.

"I have to work."

Sylvie was half listening to our conversation.

"Nothing much to do around here, kid. And you deserve a break any way."

"I'll call and ask about reservations tomorrow."

My eyes gleamed in anticipation. Whether we found any information or not, a trip out of town sounded good to me.

Chapter 7

Jeet was thrilled when he heard about the impending trip. I told him to calm down.

"Hold your horses. I haven't called them yet."

I called and asked about their cabin rentals. They offered a cabin that had two bedrooms and slept four. I booked us in for the weekend. Next week was Thanksgiving but we would be back Sunday night.

We were packed and ready to leave Friday morning. I put in half a day at work and we finally set off. Dad had reluctantly let us have the LX.

"Isn't it too cold already?" he grunted.

"We're not going camping, Dad. The cabins are heated, with TV and stuff, in case it's too cold out."

I didn't tell him about the paddle boats or the kayaks, or the outdoor swimming pool. We planned to have a blast, without parental supervision.

Motee Ba had a knowing look in her eye. She knows us too well.

"Jeet's your responsibility," she warned. "Don't let things get out of hand."

I hugged her and laughed.

"Oh Motee Ba! Do I ever? We'll be good, don't worry."

I had been a geek growing up. So okay, I had been the snarky type, but I had never gotten myself or anyone else into big trouble.

"Don't you trust me, Granny?" Tony hugged her next. "I'll have them back safe and sound."

Pappa had come out to say goodbye and wave us off. He was tapping his cane, clearing his throat, glaring at everyone.

Dad had already gone in to his books and his study.

Motee Ba was the only one who knew about the real purpose of our trip. She urged me to be sensitive to the family.

The weather for the weekend was cold and clear. Highs in the 40s were expected and the nights in the 30s. That meant some frost in the mornings, and maybe some sleet. We wouldn't get the most bang for our buck, but maybe we could meet the family and ask them some questions. I thought of Sylvie's wan face the previous evening, and strengthened my resolve to get to the bottom of Jordan Harris's death.

The ranch website said they offered three meals a day with plenty of snacks. But we had still stocked up. Food is something I never kid about. We took local two lane roads so the going was slow. Jeet had his headphones on. Becky and Tony were bickering about some latest song. I was lost in thought and an hour flew by.

"Let's stop here for a bit," Tony nudged me and I snapped out of my reverie.

There was a country store looming up and I needed a break anyway.

We used the facilities, and Tony chatted up the guy at the counter. He came back and pointed somewhere in the distance.

"Just a couple of miles now. Turn left at the sign and we're on the road to the ranch."

We piled in and Tony slowly merged onto the road. I was letting him drive. Acres of open land surrounded us. A lot of it was still green. This place deserved a visit in the summer.

I spotted the wooden hand painted sign for the Triple H ranch. Tony turned onto an unpaved road. It was smooth and well maintained, and I hoped it wouldn't mess up the suspension.

A large iron arch hung over a wooden gate announcing the Triple H. A rearing horse was placed between the two words.

The gate was wide open. They must be expecting us, I thought gladly. I always appreciate good service. Who doesn't?

Tony followed directions to a central building that was called The Lodge. There were hand painted signs at various turnoffs, showing the way to a lake, hiking trails, fishing spots and different cabins. Jeet had finally ditched his headphones and was looking around with interest.

Tony parked in front of The Lodge. A golf cart with the Triple H logo was parked in one spot. Other than that, the parking lot was empty.

We went in, looking for a front desk of sorts and came across a polished wooden counter. Keys hung on a board on the wall behind it, and a calendar had notes scribbled in. I nodded at Tony. We seemed to be in the right place.

"Hellooo," Jeet hollered, tapping an old fashioned bell.

There was no response. Jeet called out again, a bit louder this time. We heard some swearing. I noticed a small room to one side for the first time. It looked like a kind of office.

A tall, hefty man hobbled out, using a cane. Becky and I looked at each other involuntarily. He was handsome enough to make a girl swoon. His golden brown hair was cut very short. He sported a thin mustache and his blue eyes were as clear as a summer Oklahoma sky.

"We are closed!" he rasped.

I cleared my throat, but Tony beat me to it.

"We have a reservation for four. For the weekend. We are in Lake View Cottage."

The man hobbled closer and his face twisted in a sneer. Suddenly, he didn't look all that handsome.

"Didn't you hear me the first time? We are closed!"

"But we have a reservation," Becky piped up this time.

"And we got it yesterday," Tony added. "Why did you give out a reservation if you are closed?"

"Pammie!" The man roared loudly.

Loud enough for me to cover my ears with my hands.

"Damn fool woman," the man muttered, and hobbled back to his room.

We looked at each other and shrugged. I wasn't about to give up so easily. I pointed to a seating area at one side.

"Let's at least get comfortable. I'm sure someone else will turn up, other than Miss Sunshine."

I tipped my head toward the room and we giggled. Jeet and Tony grabbed a chair each and Becky and I huddled together on a sofa.

"Did you see any diner or fast food place on the way?" Jeet asked. "I'm hungry."

It was past 1 PM and we were all getting antsy. The Triple H ranch was turning out to be a Triple F, triple failure!

About ten minutes later, a door banged somewhere and we heard someone shuffle in our direction.

An older woman hurried in and went behind the desk. She glugged some water and tried to catch her breath.

She motioned me over.

"Hi! You must be Patel, party of four. Sorry but I had to step out for a few minutes. Ranch crisis, you know."

She nodded as if expecting us to understand. We nodded along.

She flipped the pages of a giant register, and asked us to fill in our details. Tony stepped forward to do the honors. Meanwhile, I gave her the once over.

The woman was in her mid thirties, dressed in a gingham dress with knee high boots. She had grayed prematurely, judging by the lines on her face. She wore a cowboy style hat. I wondered how much of her costume was for show, and whether it was really her style. She managed to look dowdy inspite of the bright red lipstick she was wearing.

"I'm Pamela Harris," she introduced herself.

A round of introductions followed as we returned the favor. She pulled a key off the board.

"Lunch is almost ready. Do y'all want to eat first or check out your cottage?"

We all wanted to eat first.

"The dining hall is around the bend. I can drive you there if you like."

We all opted for the ride. It was way past our lunch time and we were all starving. Doritos and sodas only go so far. Tony was itching to ask her about the reservation but I held him back. I wanted to get some food inside me first.

The dining room had a few round tables that seated four or six. Most of those had a 'Closed' sign over them. There was a long table that seated 10. Pamela pointed to the long table.

A young girl appeared miraculously and took our drink orders.

"We serve the same meal to everyone," Pamela explained, just as the girl came back with a tray loaded with plates. "You can let me know if you have any diet restrictions or any preferences."

Lunch was roast chicken with mashed potatoes and gravy. The girl placed bowls of steamed broccoli and corn and a big bowl of salad in the center. A tray of dinner rolls followed.

We tucked in. The food was bland but rich.

"The chicken's farm raised of course," Pamela continued as she ate with us.

The girl brought in small bowls of ice cream. We finally leaned back. I felt my mood improve. I was ready to face anything now. If they said there was no booking, I would turn away without doing anyone much harm.

Tony coughed politely before he began.

"There was a man. He said you are closed today?"

Pamela's face darkened.

"Who said that? We took your reservation, didn't we?"

"Tall, blue eyes, walks with a cane," Becky explained.

Pamela's mouth twisted in a frown.

"Ignore him. Why don't I show you to your room, er, cottage?"

She drove us back to The Lodge. We piled into the LX and followed her as she led us to our cottage for the weekend.

The road twisted a couple of times through dense greenery. We came upon a clearing. The cottage was good sized, made with some kind of wood. It set the right rustic tone. But the cottage paled in comparison to the view. A large lake stretched before us, it's water shimmering like silver in the pale sun. A cold breeze flew over the lake, making me shiver. I zipped up my fleece jacket as I looked around. We are all speechless.

"Beautiful, isn't it?" Pamela said softly.

She sounded wistful.

"Oh, I'd give anything to live here!" Becky exclaimed. She turned around and beamed at Pamela, excited. "You live here all the time?"

Pamela smiled and nodded affirmatively.

"My Daddy owns this ranch. I grew up here. And I will probably die here."

She sobered for a second and then tried to hide it.

"Let's give you a tour of the cottage."

We followed her eagerly. Any thought of Jordan Harris or investigation was farthest from my mind.

The cottage had a wide wooden porch or verandah. A patio set offered enough seating for four. I spied a hammock tied to two trees in the back. It offered a pretty view of the lake.

Pamela opened the door with the key. We entered into a small foyer that led into a great room. Spacious chairs and sofas flanked a rustic coffee table. It had a base cut out of a tree and a glass top. The place was luxurious.

A small kitchenette and bar flanked a wall. There were two bedrooms, each with their own bath. Becky and I bagged the one with a King bed. The boys were happy with the other room with two full size beds.

Pamela showed us the coffee maker.

"The fridge is stocked with creamer. You can get more coffee sachets from the lodge if you want. Dinner's at six sharp at the same place."

She turned as if to leave.

"What kind of activities do you offer?" I asked.

Pamela pointed to a file folder lying on a counter top.

"That has all the details. There's not much to do now, compared to the summer. Most guests prefer to settle in the day they arrive."

We nodded.

"Isn't there a pool here?" Jeet wanted to know.

"There's an outdoor pool but it's not heated," Pamela apologized. "We do have a hot tub on the deck in The Lodge. You can use it any time until 9 PM."

"What about tomorrow?" I asked.

Pamela smiled.

"You have our Silver package. So you pretty much call the shots. You can go kayaking or take out the paddle boats. You can get a wagon ride or a horse ride. If you want to go on a hike, we can pack a lunch for you."

Boy, were we spoiled for choice.

"I suggest you go over this binder," she pointed to the printed material. "I'll see you at six."

She got into her golf cart and sped away.

We looked around and whooped in excitement. Our camping trip hadn't turned out well this summer. Then our foliage trip had been cancelled. It had been a while since we'd had some fun. I'd worked hard through the summer, and I had money to burn. I couldn't have spent it in any better place.

Jeet jumped on the bed in his room and began flinging off his clothes.

"Who's up for a swim in that lake?" he screamed.

"The water's at least fifty degrees, you idiot. You'll freeze to death."

"Come on, Meera! Stop being such an ass!" Jeet protested.

Tony began to sneak out.

"You better not be going toward that hammock!" I ran after him and we both dove at the same time.

Luckily we collapsed into it instead of on the ground, and the thick sturdy ropes took our weight.

Becky went and sat on a small dock that reached into the water, and began reading a book.

Jeet sulked, turning the TV on full volume.

Our weekend was on in full swing.

Chapter 8

We started getting antsy by four. I made coffee and we sat in front of the TV.

"Did you notice Pamela is a Harris?" I asked. "She must be related to the guy."

"No sign of Jessica yet," Becky pointed out the obvious. "Maybe we should go looking."

"Go where? There's like a gazillion acres in this place."

"We might see her at dinner," Tony said.

"Is she even here?" I moaned.

The whole weekend suddenly seemed silly to me. Was it just going to be a big waste of money?

"Let's say Hi to Motee Ba."

I held my hand out for Tony's cell phone. Jeet ferreted out some snacks from the LX. Motee Ba had insisted we take some munchies with us, just in case. They sure came in handy.

We cleaned up and I drove the LX to the dining hall, following the directions. There were plenty of them. Someone had planned this place with care.

Pamela welcomed us and showed us to the long table. A couple of women were sitting at one of the smaller tables near a window. An older man sat slumped at another table. He looked like a poster child for a rancher, with hair that had more salt than pepper, a thick mustache and a craggy, weather beaten face. He was on the wrong side of sixty.

He nodded at us but didn't crack a smile.

"That's my dad," Pamela swung her neck toward him. "He's a bit out of sorts."

"Come meet the new guests, Pa!" she called out.

The man struggled to his feet, although he looked fitter than us.

A round of introductions followed.

"You have a nice place here, Sir," Tony said politely.

We all nodded.

"Nice? You bet it is nice." He grumbled throatily. "My boy saw to that, didn't he?"

He glared at Pamela.

"And I'm not 'out of sorts' girl. I'm thinking about my son."

His eyes shone and he shuffled back to his seat.

I found myself at a loss for words. Becky mumbled an apology and we went back and sat at our table.

"Sorry about that," Pamela said brightly. She leaned toward us and said softly. "Pa's getting a bit senile. You guys relax. Your meal will be out shortly."

"Senile?" I hissed. "The man's just lost a child, and she's calling him senile?"

My tone had alerted the two women sitting in a corner. One of them looked at us with interest.

Tony warned me to be quiet.

Dinner was served, huge platters with chicken fried steak topped with country gravy. There were large baked potatoes loaded with plenty of sour cream, bacon, chives and orange cheddar. Another bowl overflowed with fried okra. The Triple H may be giving weird vibes, but they didn't stint on food.

A warm bread pudding with plenty of raisins followed.

The blue eyed hunk from afternoon hobbled in, leaning on his cane. His face turned red when he saw us.

He pulled Pamela roughly by the arm as she came out with a flask of coffee and dragged her back into what I presumed was the kitchen.

Angry words followed.

"I'm putting a stop to this right now. It's my ranch now."

"We worked hard on this, Jordan and I," Pamela squeaked defiantly. "Where were you all this time then?"

"This will be a serious ranch now," the guy's voice rose. "None of this frippery. No more feeding people with my food."

"Shut up, Cam, these are paying customers," Pamela hissed.

"Pammie! Cam!" the older man roared.

He leaped up and strode inside.

"Shut your traps, both of you. We got company, in case you haven't noticed. Your Ma raised you better than this."

Pamela came out and mutely poured coffee. None of us dared to say a word.

"I ain't dead yet, so I'll be making any decision regarding this ranch," the old man's voice filtered through. "Now you go get your beauty sleep cuz tomorrow morning, you're taking them folks on a ride of the ranch."

A window flew open and a cold breeze came in. I shivered at some familiar feeling. Pamela walked over and shut the window.

The two other women were walking out and soon we were scraping our chairs back, wishing Pamela good night.

"Breakfast at 7 AM," she reminded us. "Dress warmly for outdoors."

"Isn't this a working ranch?" Tony wondered. "Who works the ranch?"

Pamela laughed.

"Oh. There's plenty of ranch hands and other workers. They don't eat here. This is strictly for the resort guests. We have a bunkhouse for some of the ranch hands. There are smaller cottages for the ones with families. And we have an old fashioned chuck wagon. You'll get a taste of all that tomorrow."

"I thought ranchers had to, like, get up really early," Jeet spoke up.

"They do," Pamela smiled. "We're up at 4:30 and grub's on at 5. Everyone rides out after that."

I drove the car back to our cabin. It was pitch dark without the benefit of street lights, but it was only seven in the evening.

"What do we do now?" Jeet demanded.

"How about a movie?" I asked.

The usual fight for the right tape followed and we finally settled on a scary movie.

"That hot tub sounds good right now," Tony said after a while.

We put on our swimsuits under our clothes and drove back to the lodge. We still had about thirty minutes before the 9 PM deadline. I figured that'd be enough.

The hot tub turned out to be humungous, big enough for about ten people. Everything's bigger in Texas, as they say. Technically, we were fifty or so miles shy of the Lone Star State, but the Triple H seemed to have its heart south of the border. The hot tub was occupied, but I was already freezing in my swimsuit. We walked in and cried out at the almost boiling water.

I prayed it was the older gentleman rather than the hunk but it wasn't my lucky night. He turned and nodded at us. Then he leaned back with his arms around the edge of the pool and closed his eyes. Well, two could play the game.

I wasn't going to let a sulking sour puss spoil our fun. We yapped about stuff and played around till our skin wrinkled like a prune.

Back at the cabin, we hit our beds exhausted and were out within minutes.

A few moments later, Becky was shaking me awake.

"Meera, get up. It's time for our run."

I groaned and peered out of the window. It was dark outside.

"Let's run around the lake."

I sat up in bed, rubbing my eyes.

"Why have you turned so nasty all of a sudden?" I complained.

I dragged my feet, pulled on my sweats and did a half hearted run around the lake. Becky did three laps.

Showered and dressed, we were waiting outside the dining hall at 6:45. We were all wearing jeans, boots, sweaters and jackets, along with scarves and woolen caps. It was a cold day, and there was a forecast for flurries in the afternoon.

The ranch served a full country breakfast with bacon, cheesy eggs, biscuits, sausage gravy and fluffy buttermilk pancakes. There was steak for those that wanted it.

Pamela bustled in, looking harried. She handed me a couple of printouts.

"Here's your plan for the day," she pointed out.

"A tour of the working areas of the ranch. Coffee break. A hay wagon ride after that. Mid morning snack. Horse ride. Lunch ..."

Pamela had come up with an exhausting plan for us. There didn't seem to be any time to talk to people and ask questions. I decided we would have to tag team these people, and somehow squeeze our questions in.

She walked us out just as a large truck drove up.

"You'll be riding in this. Save your fancy car."

Handsome Jerk was at the wheel. He scrambled out and smiled at us. We looked at each other. Something had changed overnight.

"Hello, I'm Cameron Harris," he introduced himself. "You can call me Cam."

We mumbled our hello, refusing to shake hands. He got the signal and withdrew his.

"I think we got off to a wrong start yesterday. It's my leg, you know. Makes me cranky."

We nodded, deciding to accept this excuse for now, although I didn't care for it much. Everyone piled into the truck and we were off.

Cam took a few turns and we came upon a hive of activity. A couple of big red barns lined the periphery. Wranglers were exercising some horses in a large corral at the center. A few other buildings were scattered around.

Cam pointed to a large whitewashed building with black shutters.

"That's the homestead. It's where we live. Pa, Pammie, Jordan and I, along with Norma, our housekeeper and cook."

"Who's Jordan?" I tried to sound disinterested.

"Er, my brother. He's not here anymore."

A couple of ranch workers tipped their hats when they saw us. We were shown the horses in their stalls. Cam pointed out the mess hall and ranch quarters, and then drove slowly through the ranch's acreage.

"This one's the easy trail," he pointed. "You can walk your horse on this in a while."

We came upon a bluff. Cam stopped the car and we got out.

"Best view on this land," he said simply.

I looked around, and wondered what it would be like to own such a vast tract of land. A couple of ponds glistened in the distance. A girl sat at the edge of a pond, throwing stones in the water. She was too far off to call out to.

Becky suddenly grabbed my hand and squeezed it dramatically. Her expression told me plenty.

"Let's see about getting you that wagon ride," Cam said and hobbled back to the car.

"Must be quite a task, maintaining all this," I began.

I had to make someone talk or the whole trip was a bust.

"Do you and Pamela do most of the work?" Tony tagged on. "Your Pa must be retired by now."

"Retired?" Cam laughed. "Anything but. No one really retires on a ranch. You work from the day you can walk until the day they bury you. It's nonstop work."

"You don't sound like you're fond of it," Becky egged.

"No. I'm not. That's why I went away. But looks like I may be destined to be a rancher after all."

"Where'd you go away?" I asked.

"I joined the Army after High School," Cam said proudly. "Sounded like the only way I could get out of shoveling manure for the rest of my life. Can't ask a man to not die for his country, you know?"

This was some twisted logic, but I guess he really hated the horses.

"I've been in the Middle East for the past few years. Then I got hit." He pointed to his leg. "My appraisal is coming up. They'll probably put me out to pasture."

"You've done your bit," Tony exclaimed. "You should be proud."

"Well, I'm barely thirty with my life stretching ahead. I don't know what I'm gonna do."

"Hey, Cowboy!" Becky snorted. "I bus tables and do dishes for a living. You are born with all this, and you're crying like a baby?"

She swung her arms around, turning in a wide circle, as if making her point.

"I know I'm luckier than most. But this was never meant to be mine."

We waited for him to continue.

"My brother Jordan, he put a lot into this ranch. This whole dude ranch thing was his idea. He wanted to do weddings, for God's sakes. And Pammie fanned the flames."

Cam was getting riled up. That was just what I wanted.

"What's wrong with the resort business? We're having a good time here."

"Too much work. And too much kissing ass. I'm not cut out for that."

"And your brother was?" I probed.

"Oh, Jordan was a ninny. He never raised his voice at anyone, never lost his temper. The ranch hands took advantage of him. So did that young chit he was going to marry. She found her meal ticket all right."

"You mean he was marrying a gold digger?" Becky asked. "Why do you rich people always think that? Maybe she was really in love."

"Has your brother gone somewhere, mister?" Jeet asked.

He could look like a cherub when he wanted to.

"Yes. Up there!" Cam pointed to the sky. "He's dead!"

We tried to act suitably surprised. We offered our apologies. And Cam drove us back for our hay wagon ride.

Chapter 9

The wagon ride was fun. It almost made me forget what we were there for. One of the wranglers gave us a brief spiel on how to handle the horses. Cam offered a ride on the gentlest mare.

"You can just ride in the corral. You don't even have to go on the walking trail. One of the men will hold the bridles and lead your horse around."

I was debating whether I wanted to risk life and limb to impress Cam. Tony and Jeet were jeering, calling me lame and some other not so nice names.

"Oh, oh!" Cam said under his breath.

We looked up to see Pamela striding toward us. She was walking fast, with a sense of purpose. Her cheeks were flaming and her mouth was set in a grim line.

"The dragon's breathing fire!" Cam warned.

Pamela pointed a finger at me, a few feet before she reached us.

"You. Meera Patel! I thought your name sounded familiar."

I acted innocent. I sensed we were about to be pushed out pretty soon.

"Hello Pamela! We're having a wonderful time." Becky gushed, trying to ease the tension.

"Yesterday, when you checked in, I was focused on getting you settled. I checked what you wrote in the book today."

"And what did they write, sister?" Cam smiled.

He had thawed a bit toward us.

"You're from Swan Creek."

She stared at us. Apparently, being from Swan Creek said it all.

"So?" Tony asked.

"Swan Creek!" Pamela said meaningfully, turning to Cameron.

He had a light bulb moment and his mouth tightened.

"And that's not all. I dug out an old newspaper. You're the one that found our Jordan."

Pamela sniffled and pointed her finger at Becky next.

"You and her! It's all in the article."

"Well, well, well …" Cam's voice had twisted in a familiar snarl.

"Thought you'd snoop some on the grieving family, eh? How much are you making out of this. A few hundred? A thousand?"

"Nobody's paying us, you idiot!" Becky burst out.

"I don't care," Pamela shrieked. "You are leaving. Now. Get your stuff and hand over your keys in the next 30 minutes."

"Wait …" I called out. "What about lunch?"

Neither of the Harris siblings gave us a ride so we walked back to The Lodge. I drove the LX to our cabin and we packed up.

"Do you think we can just not leave?" Jeet asked.

He got his answer. There was a loud knocking on the door and Pamela stood on the porch, her hands folded.

"I'll take your keys now," she thrust out her hand.

We piled into the LX and hightailed it out of the Triple H. It was 1:30 and we were starving. But none of us dared to stay behind. I had spotted the shotgun in Pamela's golf cart and no one wanted to argue with it.

"I'm starving!" Jeet complained as soon as we cleared the ranch property and merged onto the highway.

"We'll stop at the next available place," I promised.

All the activity had made us all hungry. We had healthy appetites on any day. The fresh air, the cold and the early start to the day made us all long for a hot meal.

67

Tony pointed to a sign for the country store we had stopped at earlier. It promised home-style cooking. I pulled in and we were seated. The place was small but well kept. Wooden tables and chairs looked well worn but were gleaming with polish. Lemon polish by the scent of it.

An older woman came and asked us what we wanted.

"Will y'all have lunch, or just a snack?"

"Lunch," we chorused.

"We got through our roast," the woman apologized. "I can fix some chicken and dumplings for you."

We nodded and the woman went inside. She came back with a basket of cheddar biscuits and steaming split pea soup.

"This should get you started," she smiled.

The space was a bit drafty, without central heating. Luckily, our table was placed near a wood burning fireplace.

"What a waste!" Becky groaned. "Why couldn't that Pammie have read the register a day later?"

"I was actually enjoying myself," Tony admitted.

"We did learn something, though," I pointed out.

"Like what?" Tony and Becky asked.

"Well…we confirmed Jordan was indeed a rancher. An innovative one at that. He had many ideas and a lot to look forward to."

"He didn't poison his own pie, you mean," Jeet smirked as if pointing out the obvious.

"I don't think we ever considered suicide an option," I told him, "but you're right. We can eliminate it for sure."

"What else?" Tony asked.

"He must be well to do, with such a big ranch to his name."

"We don't know that he owned the ranch," Becky pointed out. "Just that he put in a lot of work there."

"Yeah, yeah!" I said irritably. "There were three siblings, at least three that we know of. Their father's around and seemed pretty active. Jordan built this resort from the ground up. Pamela wants the resort. Cam, for some reason, doesn't want it. We don't know what he wants to do with the land, but he doesn't like the horses."

"That's quite a bit of information, once you sum it up that way," Tony agreed.

Becky's eyes widened. "And Jessica! You remember that girl by the pond? I'm sure that was her. I wanted to tell you right then."

"How can you be so sure?" I asked.

"I've seen her many times, Meera," Becky stressed. "Trust me."

"So what's she doing on the ranch?" I mused.

"Maybe she just misses the dead guy," Jeet supplied.

We took a moment to think it over and sobered. Maybe Jessica felt closer to Jordan at the ranch.

The lady brought out our food then and we tucked in. The drive back home was quiet. Tony drove and I dozed on and off, along with Jeet.

"What are you doing back so early?" Pappa demanded as we knocked on the front door.

Motee Ba's car was missing and we figured she was out with her friends. Pappa had been taking his afternoon nap in front of the TV.

"We got bored and decided to get back," I told him.

Pappa tapped his cane, muttering to himself. I heard the words 'spoiled' and 'waste of money' but I decided to ignore him. We couldn't tell him the real reason we were back anyway.

Jeet locked himself in his room and we went into mine. Becky and I slid under the covers, trying to warm up and Tony sprawled on the chair in the corner.

"What do we do now?" I began.

"Did you find it odd that the ranch still took our reservation?" Tony asked.

I looked at him inquiringly.

"Well, it's barely a week since they lost their son. Shouldn't they be shut down? What are they doing, serving meals to people, entertaining them."

Becky sat up straighter.

"And it wasn't just us. There were those women too. I could get it if our booking was old and they were honoring it. But we called two days ago, remember?"

"Some people prefer to stay busy," I said lamely. "Maybe that helps them deal with the grief."

"Grief?" Becky smirked. "That Pamela wasn't grieving at all. She called her father senile, remember?"

"What about that guy, hunh?" Tony asked. "He was too flippant."

"Maybe they need the money. Some people don't turn away paying customers."

I tried to give them the benefit of doubt.

"A month after the fact, I can agree to all your arguments, Meera," Tony said seriously. "But not in a week."

"So do you think any of these could be involved?" I asked outright.

"My money's on that Pamela. Shriveled up old prune."

Becky had taken a dislike to the woman. That much was clear. Tony disagreed.

"I pick Cameron. He can probably use a gun, and very well. He seemed bitter."

"But Jordan was supposedly poisoned," I objected. "I don't see a soldier using that as a weapon."

"What about Jessica?" Becky reminded us. "Cameron called her a gold digger, remember?"

"What was she doing getting engaged anyway? Isn't she too young?" I mused.

"She's getting her doctorate. She's the same age as us, Meera. Maybe older. People do get married in college, you know."

There was a sudden silence as we all digested this.

Tony cleared his throat.

"It's OK!" he held up his palm. "It's bound to come up sometime or the other. You don't have to walk on eggshells around me."

Tony's marriage is a subject as painful as my mother. Probably more. These are the two things we avoid talking about at all costs.

I buried my head in my pillow. The maze was getting more twisted.

"Check this, Meera," Tony said. "We have a list of people who were closely related to Jordan Harris. There may be more but this is a beginning."

"Yeah," Becky pointed on her fingers. "Old man Harris, Pamela, Cameron and Jessica. And that Norma woman we never saw."

"Well, let's not forget the ranch hands either," I insisted. "Maybe one of them had a beef with Jordan. Maybe they argued over money, or had a falling out. There's too many people on that ranch."

"I agree," Tony said. "But let's concentrate on the people closest to him for now."

"We really need to talk to Jessica," I said.

"She may be at school tomorrow," Becky said hopefully. "Or maybe she won't be back until after the Thanksgiving break."

"I'll walk over there tomorrow and try to talk to her," I offered.

"I can fill Sylvie and Jon in on what happened," Becky added.

"Did you notice those two women?" I asked Tony.

"What women?" he spread his hands wide.

Tony hardly ever notices any girl above the age of 25.

"How old do you think Pamela must be?" Becky mused. "She looked old, didn't she?"

I shrugged.

"Old and bitter," Tony said. "I wonder if she's one of the H in Triple H. Or if there's another one."

"How do you mean?" I asked.

"Well, land generally passes to the son, or sons. It all depends on when the ranch was named."

"You're such a chauvinist," I complained.

"It is what it is," Tony said, rolling his eyes. "All I'm sayin' is, we don't know."

"Maybe Harris is her married name?" Becky speculated. "She could be a widow."

I shut my eyes and lined up all their faces in my mind. Pamela had the same sharp aquiline nose of the old man. Her blue eyes were a bit cloudy, but they were the same shade as Cam's.

"Nah!" I shook my head. "I think she's a Harris by birth."

Becky yawned and that set us all off. Tony and Becky left and I gave in to an afternoon nap.

I sat at the kitchen counter, sipping Chai with Motee Ba later that evening.

"Any progress?" she asked simply.

"Yes and No," I said. "We know more than we did before."

"That's always good," Motee Ba nodded sagely.

The phone rang and we suffered yet another setback. Sylvie was on the phone, sounding frantic. Motee Ba was trying to calm her down.

"They just sealed the diner," she told me after she hung up.

She was slightly out of breath, and a few beads of perspiration mottled her brow.

"What do you mean, sealed? Who can do that?"

"The Health Department," Motee Ba spat. "Or whatever they are called in Swan Creek."

"But why?" I cried out.

"Someone reported rats. So now they are going to search the place for rodents and for any toxins lying about."

"That's ridiculous!" I was in shock.

I knew how troubled Jon and Sylvie already were. This was going to be worse.

"You need to step up your efforts, Meera," Motee Ba pointed out the obvious.

Chapter 10

I spent most of Sunday sleeping and reading. That's pretty much all you can do after gorging on Motee Ba's mutton curry. It was the only bright spot in an otherwise dreary weekend. Motee Ba had invited Jon and Sylvie to come over, but they had opted out.

The campus was quiet, it being Thanksgiving week. Most locals head home, and others have flights out sometime in the week. The international students stay put, unless they receive an invite from some American they have befriended. Dead Week, that dreaded week before the exams was looming, and kids were huddled at tables all across the library. Last minute group study sessions, project reports and exams were being discussed.

I caught a break around 11 and walked over to the engineering building. I had done some digging around on the college network and found Jessica had office hours at this time. I located her office and knocked on the door. I half expected someone else to be subbing for her.

"Come in," a voice called out softly.

I entered and came face to face with a young girl. I had never met her before so there was no way to tell if this was indeed Jessica.

The girl was about my age. Her face was scrubbed clean, devoid of makeup. There were purple patches under her eyes, which were slightly swollen. Judging by the pile of Kleenex on her desk, she'd been indulging in a sob session.

"Are you Jessica?" I asked.

She nodded.

"You were at the ranch earlier, right?"

I was glad she got to the point. I had no idea how I was going to explain my presence in her office.

"Pamela's still fuming. Why were you there anyway?"

I sat down.

"We just wanted to meet you and offer our condolences."

"That's bull."

She was blunt even in her grief.

"It's like this. I work at Sylvie's, you know, the diner over on the highway?"

"I know the place," Jessica said simply.

"Sylvie and Jon are like family. My friend Becky works there full time. I just play around with recipes."

"What can I do for you?" Jessica asked with interest.

"People are talking. They are saying Sylvie's pie killed your boyfriend. They're losing business."

Jessica had a faraway look in her eyes. I wondered if she had tuned me out. I cleared my throat, hoping to get her attention.

"I'm listening," she said.

"I promised Sylvie I would help her."

"Are you some kind of detective?" she asked curiously.

"Not really," I blushed. "It's like this. Earlier this year, I was trying to find a missing girl. Just by chance, I also solved a murder."

Jessica sat up straighter.

"Are you the one who found Prudence Walker's killer?"

I nodded.

"Sort of."

"You must be good."

I shrugged. I didn't know what I was doing. I had stumbled upon the culprit last time while looking for a missing Indian girl. This time, I just wanted to clear Sylvie's name.

"I just want to help Sylvie. And we figure the only way to do that is find out what really killed Jordan. Or who did."

"You think the family's involved?" Jessica asked cannily.

"I don't know. I'm not saying they are. But talking to them seems like the first step."

A tear rolled down Jessica's face.

"He was a good man. My Jordan. He didn't deserve this."

I saw a window of opportunity.

"Would you be willing to help me?"

"Any way I can," Jessica said eagerly. "Ask me anything. I'll do my best to answer your questions. And I'll tell you everything there is to know about Jordan Harris."

"You realize I have to consider you a potential suspect too, right?" I asked. "It's just part of the process."

"Fire away. I have nothing to hide."

Jessica took a sip of water from a bottle on her desk. I pulled out a writing pad from my bag.

"So let's start with you," I began. "Tell me something about yourself. Where are you from? How long have you been in Swan Creek? Something of that sort."

"I'm from Texas," Jessica smiled. "Just over the Oklahoma border. My Daddy has a ranch there. A working cattle ranch with a couple of thousand acres. I always wanted to go to college. Swan Creek has great bio technology research. I am working on my doctoral thesis, hoping to finish by next year."

I nodded.

"So where'd you meet Jordan? In some ranching circles?"

Jessica looked surprised.

"Right here, in Swan Creek. He went to Pioneer."

"I didn't know Jordan was an alumnus!" I wondered how this tiny detail had never come up.

Jessica nodded.

"We met in freshman year. He finished his classes in three years. He commuted while doing his thesis. By that time, he had taken on a lot of responsibility over at the Triple H."

"Freshman year?" I was impressed. "That seems like a long time ago.

"About 7 years," Jessica said glumly. "We were both on a fast track. I stayed on to do my master's and doctoral work, of course. But we were still in touch."

"Becky said you were celebrating your engagement that day?"

Jessica looked wistful.

"He had already proposed. Down by the pond over at his ranch. It was so romantic. We just wanted to get away for a meal. Have a change of scene. He wanted to take me to some fancy restaurant in OKC, but I said Swan Creek was cool. I had to get back and put in a few hours at the lab that night."

"What happened after your dinner?"

"We went to Willow Springs, of course!"

I understood.

Willow Springs, our local lake, is one of the few attractions in our small town. It's a choice hangout spot for the college kids, and for couples looking for a romantic setting.

"The moon was out, and it was too cold for the usual barbecues and parties. It was perfect!"

I waited for her to go on. Silence often spurs the other person to talk, rather than a direct question.

"We talked about our future. Jordan had big plans for the Triple H. Then I had to leave."

"Did you drive back on your own?" I couldn't imagine them going to a romantic date in two cars.

"I caught a ride," Jessica said. "Jordan wanted to sit there for a while. I had a meeting back at the lab at 8:30."

Talking about some dry research topic at 8:30 on a Sunday night? This is the kind of stuff that made me drop out of grad school. These people need to get a life.

"Did you talk to him again later?" I was getting close to the wire.

"I did. Jordan called me around 10. I was just coming out of my meeting. He said he had dozed off on the bench. But he was getting ready to go home."

"Did he, er, not stay with you?"

Jessica frowned.

"Very rarely. Jordan was very prim and proper. And he had an early start at the ranch every day. He preferred to drive home if the weather was good."

"You didn't insist he spend the night?"

I tried to imagine them. Say I had just been on a romantic date with the person I was going to spend my life with. Wouldn't I want to stay over?

"I was planning an allnighter. I have to submit a research paper for a conference. I am already behind schedule. I was going to slog all of last week and then we would have Thanksgiving Week to ourselves."

I was stumped. I thought hard about my next question.

"Did he like pie?"

Jessica's eyes filled up again.

"Yes! Especially the one at Sylvie's. He couldn't eat nuts, but he always went there for her berry pie. She always set some aside for him."

"Did he get along with his family?"

Jessica thought a bit.

"He looked up to the old man. The ranch was everything to him. It flourished under his management. He planted some crops. There were the horses and then the resort. He built that from the ground up."

"What about the siblings?"

"Pamela's a spinster. She's always lived with them. He was fine with that."

"She seemed quite efficient," I observed.

"The resort gave her new life. She loved talking to the guests, adding a woman's touch. She was totally on board with Jordan's plans for expanding the resort."

"What about that sour puss?" I crinkled my nose.

Jessica frowned.

"Cam? Now Cam's a surprise."

I looked at her inquiringly.

"He hated the ranch. Still hates it. He went away and joined the Army. Now he's back, facing a discharge."

"What did Jordan feel about the prodigal brother?"

"Nothing much to feel. He's family. It's his inheritance as much as Jordan's and Pam's."

"So Jordan was okay with Cam coming back to stay on the ranch?"

"I guess. I didn't want to interfere."

"And the old man?"

"Oh, Pa Harris? He's such a dear. He grew up on that land. He was very happy with the changes Jordan made. He as good as signed over everything to Jordan."

"I bet the other two weren't pleased?"

Jessica was quiet.

"You don't think Jordan died because of money, do you?"

"Hard to say anything at this point," I quipped. "I'm just trying to get as much information as possible."

"My Daddy's rich. Super rich." Jessica looked sad. "And I'm an only child. It will all come to me one day."

"And did Jordan know that?"

"I suppose," Jessica mused. "It was kinda obvious, although we never talked about it. Jordan was the proud sort. He wanted to make it on his own. The land wasn't his, of course. But everything else was."

"How was his state of mind last week. Was he happy, sad, troubled about something? Angry?"

"You don't think he harmed himself, do you?" Jessica demanded. "Jordan would never do that. He had big plans. We were planning our wedding for next summer, after my graduation."

"He must have been feeling something," I probed further.

Jessica was silent for a while. I rode it out.

"He was a bit worried about Cam," she finally admitted. "He didn't know what to expect from him."

"How do you mean?"

"Cam never hid the fact that he hated the ranch. One day he would talk about selling off the land. Then he would want to plant wheat on all the acres. Then he wanted to plant an organic farm."

"Did they fight over it?"

"Not in front of me," Jessica shook her head. "Cam was unpredictable. You never knew what fancy plan he might come up with next."

I had a lot to process. And I couldn't think of any more questions.

"That's all I can think of right now. But I may want to ask you more questions later."

Jessica wrote down a number on a Post-It note. She slid it over to me.

"This is my number, and my email. Feel free to get in touch any time. I'll do anything to help you get to the bottom of this."

"Um, about that," I ventured. "Do you think you could get me back on the ranch? I would like to talk to the rest of the family."

"I'll see what I can do," Jessica promised.

I walked back to my desk and spent the rest of the day on my feet. I drove to the diner, knowing it was closed. There was a big fat seal across the entrance. A callous flyer informed whoever concerned that the property was closed for inspection.

Becky sat on a stoop, looking morose. She had been waiting for me.

"Where's Jon and Sylvie?" I asked.

"Haven't seen them today. I spoke to Jon on the phone. Sylvie's been crying her eyes out. They are afraid they might lose their license."

"I didn't realize it was that serious."

I was trying to figure out what was wrong.

"We work here every day, Becky. We know there's no rats in there. Or any rat poison. Maybe we shouldn't be worried."

"Reputation is everything in the food business," Becky lamented. "Even if the department clears the place, people will still remember it was shut down."

"We'll deal with that when the time comes," I sighed. "Let's go!"

Chapter 11

The campus was like a deserted town in an old Western movie
on Wednesday afternoon. I drove straight home. Tony was busy
running errands for his mom. We were all invited to
Thanksgiving dinner at the Sinclairs'. We've split up holidays
between us so everyone can enjoy. We do Labor Day and Diwali,
and Aunt Reema has us over for Thanksgiving. Her menu is
always a mix of traditional Thanksgiving dishes with some of her
Indian recipes.

I was making my cranberry relish. It was the only dish we were
taking to the party. Sylvie was expected to bring a couple of pies,
but I wasn't sure she would be up to it in her current frame of
mind.

I had chosen to cook the cranberries in our guest house. This is
like a spacious apartment right on our property, a few feet away
from the main house. It's a great hang out spot for us when
we're in a rowdy mood. I like to use the kitchen there for trying
out new recipes. It's one of the few places where I can be alone
and undisturbed.

I switched off the burner and lifted the pot containing the spicy
berries onto a cold one. I was looking forward to a few hours of
solitude.

I settled down on the deep leather couch that looked out onto
the patio. I closed my eyes, and took a few deep breaths, trying
to clear my mind of all thought. I had put this off long enough,
but it was high time I embarked on my personal project.

The last memory I have of my mother is walking back home
from school, holding her hand, begging for cookies. On that
fateful day, Swan Creek was struck by a freak tornado and it
ripped off more than the roof of our house. My mother, Sarla
Patel, was a casualty of this F-3 that wreaked havoc in our lives.
She was never seen or heard of again, declared dead by the State
after the required number of years.

Jeet and I were raised by Motee Ba and Pappa. Dad was more an absentee father, buried in his books and his research. Anything related to Mom has been taboo in our family. Until this summer. My search for a hapless Indian student had stirred the pot, riling us all up. I had finally dared to confront Dad, and voice all my anguish related to my mother. I learned how hard they had worked to track her down. I was able to forgive my Dad a bit. But a new resolve had developed in my mind.

I vowed to try and find my Mom, dead or alive. Maybe I am being foolish. What do I know, after all? The trail was cold, seventeen years later. I was setting myself up for failure.

The first time I'd mentioned this, Tony had looked at me like I was crazy. Jeet, that stupid teen brother of mine, had been ready to burst into tears. That had only strengthened my resolve and told me one thing. I had to do this on my own.

I considered the type of investigations that had already been done. Right after the accident, police had checked the neighboring states for any casualties. Mom's photograph had probably been faxed over to surrounding police stations. I didn't know exactly what had been done. But there was a good chance some new information had surfaced in the last seventeen years.

I fired up the computer and tried to find some information online. I was trying to find out if there was some kind of database for unsolved cases. I wanted to check if Mom's name was still on there. If not, I wanted to put it there.

One of the first things anyone would need was a photograph. I imagined approaching people with a twenty year old photo. It just wouldn't fly. I needed to get a brief idea of what Mom would look like today.

I wrote my first task down. Find out what Mom would look like today. Image processing was one of my favorite subjects in college. I had played around with a lot of morphing software. Now I needed to write a program that would add age to a photo. It would take a few days but I could do it.

The hard part was getting in touch with the right authorities, asking them stuff. I wrote down the scenarios that had been already considered. Death! No body had ever turned up and this gave me hope.

Dad had told me about another scenario they had thought of. What if my mother did not want to be found? I decided to table it for the time being.

What if Mom had been hurt or injured, unable to speak or tell someone about herself? Maybe she had been held against her will? I forced myself to think about worst case situations, however dire they sounded. The alternative was my Mom didn't exist. Anything was better than that.

Contacting the authorities was going to be the next step. I needed to check if there was any active missing persons report about Mom. If not, I probably had to open one. I realized I couldn't do all this on the sly. I needed to discuss this with Dad and Motee Ba. It wasn't a conversation I was looking forward to.

Writing an aging program was something I could do without anyone's help. I got started on it right away.

Everyone woke up late on Thursday. I made pumpkin pancakes and served them with a special spiced syrup. I add ricotta to the batter and these pancakes are really heavy. So okay, we would stuff ourselves at Thanksgiving dinner but that would be much later around 3 or 4 PM. A hearty brunch was in order.

Cheesy scrambled eggs with jalapenos went great with the pancakes, topped with fresh salsa and sour cream.

I had come to a decision last night. I was going to level with Dad from the onset. I decided to confront him right after brunch.

Dad had disappeared into his study the minute he finished shoveling his breakfast. Half the time, I doubt if he even notices what he eats. I knocked on the study door, bracing myself for a tough talk.

"Come in, Meera!" he called out.

Dad can always tell who's at the door.

"That brunch was excellent," he complimented.

I smiled.

"How much trouble are you in?" he joked.

"I want to reopen Mom's case," I blurted out.

Dad's face turned a shade darker.

"How do you mean?"

"I want to look for her, Dad. I need this."

He was quiet for a minute.

"I thought you might get around to this someday."

"Look, Dad. I'm glad you told me about all your efforts. I have no doubt you did your best. The best that was possible at that time. But it's been, what, seventeen years. New information could have come to light."

"So you'll look for her now," Dad began. "And what? Look again 20 years later? Who knows how far technology will advance in the next 20 years?"

I thought that was unfair, but I stuck to my point.

"I need to do this now. Reopen the case. Talk to people."

"What do you want from me?" he asked, sounding old.

"Your blessing," I answered. "I don't want to hide anything from the family. And I need you to help me with any questions that might arise."

"Alright," Dad said. "I'm with you. But remember one thing, Meera. You'll have to face the truth, whatever it is."

I told myself I was ready for that. I went around his desk and hugged Dad.

"I'm writing a program that will show age progression," I told him.

His eyes gleamed.

"Why didn't I think of that?" he slapped his head.

"I need an old photo, or a few old photos to work with."

"By all means," Dad said cheerfully. "Use the scanner here. Scan them in."

I smiled. We were supposed to be intelligent. We could achieve a lot if we put our heads together.

Dad read my mind.

"You know what, Meera? Maybe fresh eyes on this is a good thing. And everyone might come up with something different. Something they missed at that time, either because they were too close to it, or because they were grieving. I think you should start by interviewing Pappa, Ba and me."

I was amazed. I had decided to broach this at some other time, but Dad had made it easy for me.

"And," he said, stooping down with a bunch of keys, "take this."

He unlocked a drawer and pulled out a binder that was at least 10 inches thick.

"This has all the information – reports we filed, reports sent in by the investigator I hired, missing people organizations we contacted, newspapers we put ads in. Review this first."

"Thanks Dad," I teared up. "This should be a good starting point."

"I suggest you still redo all that, since we want to start fresh. But this way you'll know what was tried last time and what wasn't."

I had gone in expecting a big argument. Instead, Dad had handed me a treasure trove of information.

"Today's Thanksgiving, isn't it?" Dad mused. "It's kind of fitting that you embark on this today."

Giving Dad one more big hug, I scrambled out. I decided to call a family meeting right then. I summoned Jeet to the living room. Motee Ba & Pappa were already there, watching the Thanksgiving Day Parade on TV.

"I have an announcement!" I plunged ahead.

I gave them the short version of what I proposed to do.

"Good luck, sweetie. I hope you succeed."

Motee Ba had teared up as expected. Jeet looked resigned.

"I'll pitch in if needed, Meera."

He had been barely two when we lost Mom. He didn't remember her at all.

Pappa tapped his cane, getting excited. I thought he would blow a fuse.

"Finally you're talking sense, girl," he sputtered. "I've been waiting for you to grow up and go look for your mother."

This was my second shock of the day.

"Why didn't you say something all this time, Pappa?" I burst out.

"Waiting for you to grow up, wasn't I?" he growled.

"Hush, Mr. Patel," Motee Ba warned, fearing an argument.

She held out her arms and I went into them, sitting on the edge of her chair. Jeet rolled his eyes, made a gagging sound and disappeared into his room.

We piled into the LX a few hours later, ready to go to Tony's for dinner. I pulled him aside as soon as Aunt Reema welcomed us into their beautiful home.

I gave Tony the lowdown, waiting for him to say something.

"I'm with you, Meera!" he said, kissing the top of my head. "I'll help in any way you want."

The doorbell rang and Sylvie and Jon came in. Sylvie was slightly out of breath, but she looked happy. I was amazed. Maybe she'd started on the wine a bit early.

"Sorry we're late," she said, handing over a couple of pies to Aunt Reema. "Last minute order for some pies."

My eyes met Tony as we mulled over this surprising development. But the smells from the kitchen soon drew us in. After multiple servings of turkey and fixings, we went out to play football. Dad joined us for a while, then the grownups dozed in front of the TV.

Becky drove up and I filled her in again on the latest. We went in for pie and a game of Monopoly, enjoying the holiday.

Chapter 12

Dead Week arrived with its usual chaos. Kids were scrambling to send in their final projects and papers. There wasn't an inch of free space in the library. Every chair was taken and in some places, kids squatted on the carpeted floors, peering over notes and books.

I was feeling a bit nostalgic. We've all been there, haven't we? Moaning over why we wasted the entire semester partying or lazing around, promising ourselves the next time would be better. And the four years just flew by like that, at the snap of your fingers.

I dragged myself home, exhausted. I had a bit of a headache and all I wanted was some peace and quiet.

"Message for you," Motee Ba announced as soon as I entered through the kitchen. "Someone called Cam. Wants you to call him back."

"Cameron Harris?" I exclaimed. "That's the dead guy's brother. We met him at the ranch."

"Seems like a handsome brother, judging by the look on your face," Motee Ba said cagily.

I blushed.

I took the number Motee Ba offered and went into my room. I dialed the number, wondering why the sour puss was calling me.

"Hello?" A voice answered hesitantly.

I recognized Cam's voice. He sounded a bit uncertain.

"This is Meera. Meera Patel. I'm just returning your call."

"Oh, Hi!" his voice came on clear. "Yes, I did call and leave a message. How are you?"

We exchanged some pleasantries. All the time I was wondering what he wanted from me.

"Jessica mentioned you're looking into Jordan, er, Jordan's death," he said after a pause. "And that you wanted to talk to the family."

"That's right," I confirmed.

"Well, I don't know about Pa or Pammie, but I'm ready to meet with you and answer any questions you may have."

"That's great," I stopped lounging and sat up in bed. "Do you want me to come to the ranch?"

"Not necessary. I'm coming that way tomorrow. How about we meet for lunch. Or an early dinner?"

I didn't think I could get away from my desk, so I picked dinner. I suggested the Thai place and he agreed readily.

"How about 5:30 then?" I asked.

I didn't have a free moment all day the next day. Lunch was just a pre-packed salad I picked up from a campus store. I was starving by the time I entered the Thai place.

Cam was waiting, leaning on his cane. The hostess showed us to a table, greeting me with familiarity. I was on friendly ground.

There was an awkward moment as we both tried to make small talk. Then Cam shook his head and leaned closer.

"Ask anything you want. I have nothing to hide. And I want to find out what happened to my little brother."

"I'm not sure how much Jessica told you," I lead. "Sylvie and Jon are…"

Cam waved a hand as if trying to rush me.

"I know all that. No need to explain. Why don't we get on with the questions?"

I sensed the cranky sourpuss surfacing. He slumped suddenly and looked ashamed.

"Look, I'm sorry. I don't mean to be rude. It's this blasted leg, see. It starts hurting suddenly, and once that happens, I can't keep a thought straight in my head. That's why I want you to get to the point. We don't have much time."

I assured him I understood. Or did I?

"Are you older than Jordan?" I led with something simple.

Cam leaned back and a nostalgic look came over his face.

"Yes. He was the baby of the family. Pam's the oldest of course. I came by almost 10 years later. And then Jordan was born."

"You must've been close, being almost the same age."

Cam nodded.

"That we were. Didn't have much choice in playmates, did we? Growing up on the ranch? Not too many neighbors."

"Did you always dislike life at the ranch?" I asked.

"Was never too fond of it," Cam agreed readily. "I wanted to get out, see the world. I grabbed my chance soon as I graduated."

"And now you've come back."

I stated the obvious.

"At least for a while, yes. Although this whole thing with Jordan has put me in a tight spot."

"How so?" I asked.

"I came to recuperate at the ranch. Pa insisted. It's actually a bit inconvenient for me, driving over to the city all the time to get my check ups."

"So you weren't planning to stay?"

Cam shook his head.

"Didn't I say I was eager to get away? Why would I go back there? I had an apartment all picked out in Dallas. Got a couple of old Army buddies there who were going to set me up in a cushy job."

"So ranching was never your thing then?"

"No sireee, it wasn't," Cam repeated, slurping the Tom Kha soup the waitress had finally brought over.

"Jessica mentioned you wanted to start an organic farm on the ranch?"

Cam looked sheepish.

"Oh that? That was just a thought. I was having a bit of fun with Jordan."

"You mean you were purposely needling him?"

Cam shrugged.

"You like picking fights, don't you?" I didn't hide my acerbic tone.

"Hey, I was just hanging around. Nothing much to do at the ranch. Jordan and Jessica were right there, canoodling all the time, talking about their future, going on and on about their big plans. It was all a bit too much."

He made a gagging motion with his hands.

"You mean you were jealous."

"A bit," he agreed. "Mostly I was feeling sorry for myself. It's this leg, like I told you."

He pointed to his foot and pulled up his trouser leg. I got a glimpse of a prosthetic. I hadn't realized how serious his injury was earlier.

"Sometimes, the pain is so severe. I'll do anything to distract myself, keep myself from crying out."

"So you picked fights with your siblings."

Somehow, I wasn't feeling too sympathetic toward Cameron

Harris. He was a lesson in how looks can be deceiving. Those baby blues of his had stopped having any effect on me.

"Do you ride?" I asked.

I was getting tired. I needed to fill time to think of some more questions.

"A couple of hours every day. I did grow up on a ranch after all."

He smiled in what may be called an engaging manner.

"So the ranch is not all that bad, hunh?"

"The place was beginning to grow on me, to be honest."

"Did you tell anyone about it?"

Cameron looked uncomfortable.

"They had this pretty life. All of them did. Pa had almost signed over the ranch to Jordan. He was getting married. Pammie was happy running that dude ranch business. They didn't really want me there."

"And now?" I asked softly.

"Now it's all up in the air. Pa's getting old. He was looking forward to taking it easy."

"So you might be able to convince him to turn the ranch into an organic farm. Or plant on all 500 acres."

"I see Jessica's been talking," he sneered.

The sourpuss was beginning to surface again.

"What changed your mind?" I asked. "About the ranch?"

"It's so peaceful," Cam's tone was wistful. "It began to grow on me. I'm a bit battle weary. I've seen too much evil to last one lifetime."

"I would think it would be perfect after the stressful life you've led."

Cam's eyes widened.

"I thought of that. It's actually great for soldiers who need an extended convalescence. We already have the infrastructure for that, with the cabins. We can build more."

I was a bit confused.

"So all your other business ideas – the organic farm, the wheat crop – they were just a fib?"

"I was trying to gauge their reaction. See if they were conducive to something I suggested. How they felt about me staying on."

"And all this time you actually wanted to turn the Triple H into a fancy spa for wounded soldiers."

"Not exactly, but in a nutshell, yes."

Cam's face had brightened, and he was staring into some future I wasn't privy to.

"Just think about what we have to offer – fresh air, farm grown fresh food, the lake, the ponds, and the horses! Think of all the therapy they can offer to trauma victims. And to folks who are disabled like me."

"Have you discussed this with anyone yet?" I asked.

Cam shook his head.

"It's too soon. The ranch isn't going anywhere."

Now that Jordan was dead, it certainly wasn't.

"Couldn't you have done both? Let Jordan operate the resort and the dude ranch, and reserved some of the space for the sick people?"

Cam shrugged.

"I guess."

I pushed aside my plate of Pad Thai noodles. I thought of all the Agatha Christie books I had read, and the cop shows Pappa continuously watched on TV.

Cam seemed to have a motive, if having the ranch to himself was one. Of course, Pamela was still around, and she probably had a share in the ranch. But maybe she would just fall in line with what her brother wanted.

Did Cam have an opportunity to harm Jordan?

"Where were you that Sunday, when Jessica and Jordan were celebrating their engagement?"

He gave me a devilish grin.

"Want to know if I did it? Why don't you just ask me outright?"

I squirmed. I guess my question had been obvious.

"I was in the city," he said. "I urged them to come with me, you know. I told Jordan he should take her to a nice steakhouse in the city. Not some old diner they could go to any time."

I opened my mouth to object. He beat me to it.

"Nothing wrong with the diner, but I'm sure it's not the place for a romantic date."

I tried to picture myself on a date. I had a sparkling diamond on my finger. I wanted to show it off. Where would I want to be? I would want flowers and candles, and table cloths. As much as I loved Sylvie's, it was too down home for such an occasion.

"I get that," I admitted. "Jessica said she had some meeting at Pioneer."

Cam rolled his eyes.

"Couldn't she have bowed out of it? How many times do you celebrate your engagement, hunh?"

"So you went to the city," I steered Cam to the point. "Oklahoma City, right?"

"I had a doctor's appointment at 4. And then I had a session with my therapist. It was almost 8 PM by the time I started back.

Had to grab dinner from a drive through."

Cam could have been in Swan Creek sometime around 10. Jordan was still around here at that time.

"I had no need to come into Swan Creek," he said, snapping me out of my thoughts. "Far as I knew, Jordan was already home and in his bed."

"But he wasn't," I stated the obvious. "Can you think of any reason why he may have stuck around?"

Cam looked uncomfortable.

"I don't know."

He was hiding something, but I didn't want to push him.

"When did you notice he wasn't around?"

"I don't think anyone did," he told me. "Pammie's the one who locks up at night, after dinner and stuff. I think a couple of cabins were rented out that week. Jordan gets up at 4 and has grub with all the ranch hands around 5. They would notice his absence. But most people knew about his big date. I guess they thought he overslept."

"So ... no one missed him until the cops called?"

I tried to imagine Dad taking that kind of a call. Especially when he thought I was in my room sleeping.

"Must've been a shock," I said softly. "For everyone."

"Pa's the one most affected," Cam said quietly. "Although you wouldn't know it, looking at him."

"So, did he have any enemies?" I asked.

"Jordan was the sweetest guy you'd ever meet. He was kind to everyone. Never thought he'd come to a sticky end."

"What about Jessica? Did they get along well?"

"Have you been listening at all?" Cam frowned. "They just got engaged, didn't they? Why would they get hitched if they didn't get along?"

"I don't know. I'm just trying to cover all the bases."

"Shooting in the dark, hoping you'll hit some target?" Cam smirked.

I realized I was doing exactly that. Cam was rubbing his leg, getting antsy.

"You've been pretty helpful, Cam."

I thanked him and he agreed to get in touch if he thought of anything more. I watched him drive off and got into my Camry. I reached home 10 minutes later. I spotted Sylvie's car outside the guest house. I found her in the kitchen, rolling out pie dough.

The diner was out of commission and we still had plenty of leftovers from Thanksgiving. I wondered who she was cooking for.

"What's this?" I raised my eyebrows.

"We have a standing order for 10 pies every day," Sylvie beamed.

She pulled out two lattice pies from the oven and set them on the counter to cool. The cherry filling oozed out, filling the air with a heady, sweet aroma.

"Are you allowed to make these?" I asked, confused about the legalities.

"I can't use the diner kitchen. But I can cook if I want. And I can make a pie if I want to."

She sounded defiant.

"Someone from town?" I asked.

Sylvie hummed along with the radio, pouring some toasted pecans into a pie plate lined with crust. Either she didn't hear me or she didn't want to say.

I wondered about this sudden demand for Sylvie's pies in Swan Creek.

Chapter 13

The meeting with Cam left me with an uncomfortable feeling. There was something not quite right about him. Maybe it was some sixth sense, or just prejudice.

I checked out some image processing books from the library and read up on it in my spare time. I started working on my program. That was the easy part. Going through the thick binder Dad had given me was the tough one. Every time I opened the file, I got lost in some minute detail and found myself tearing up. This way, I would never make any progress. I thought of asking Tony for some help.

Finals Week started and the campus emptied a bit every day. I was on pancake duty for two nights. This is a tradition at Pioneer. The library, along with the alumni office serves pancakes at midnight every day during the exams. Students line up for the food and a much needed break from their heavy duty studying. I suppose the sugar keeps them going until morning.

I had flipped my thousandth pancake and was ready to call it quits when I held up a plate for the next person in line. I found myself staring at Jessica.

"I'm gonna miss these pancakes when I graduate," she said wistfully. "They're tradition, you know."

I nodded.

Jessica took the plate from my hands and leaned forward to whisper softly.

"I talked to Pamela and Pa Harris. They will talk to you. You have to go to the ranch, though."

I blinked to let her know I understood. She was edged out by the next person in line.

Two days later, I was riding in Tony's truck, on the way to the Triple H. I had put in a lot of overtime and I was due half a day.

We had decided to go and talk to Pamela and Mr. Harris.

"Did you talk to Stan lately?" Tony asked, cruising along at the speed limit of 50 miles per hour.

"Yeah. He came home yesterday."

"Do they have any more news about Jordan? Like his cause of death?"

"That's the curious thing."

I poured out what Stan Miller had told me the earlier day.

"So he died a natural death?" Tony asked incredulously. "Why are we going to interview his family, then?"

"They are not sure," I said uncertainly. "Stan said something about him being in shock, but there not being sufficient proof. They don't know what brought it on. And in the absence of anything definite, they just might call it an accident. Or something like that."

"And they say science has advanced!" Tony smirked.

"I guess some questions are tough to answer," I tried to be philosophical.

"So he wasn't poisoned then?"

I shook my head.

"Not by the usual means. If he was poisoned, it was something untraceable."

"Like some strange foreign virus, you mean?" Tony asked, bewildered.

"I'm as clueless as you are, Tony. But our goal is to prove it wasn't the pie. Or rather, it wasn't Sylvie's pie."

"Wasn't Sylvie's pie found on him?" Tony sounded frustrated.

"Yes, but maybe someone doctored it. Doused it with something when he wasn't looking?"

"Yeah. Yeah. When he went for a swim in that lake I suppose."

I folded my arms and looked away. Tony could be really indelicate at times.

Some flurries started blowing and the sky darkened. I cranked up the heat in the truck. Tony drove through the arches of the Triple H and pulled up outside The Lodge. Pamela was meeting us there at 3. It was ten to.

I shivered as I rushed up the steps. Tony put his arm around me, but I gently pushed it away. I was still mad at him for the snarky comment.

Pamela Harris was standing behind the check-in desk when we entered. She ushered us to a seating area near the window. She seemed restless and I wondered if Cam had railroaded her into doing this.

"You know what the police are saying?" she burst out. "They're saying Jordan died naturally. They're just a bunch of lazy country bums."

I was surprised to see Pamela display so much emotion. Maybe she would be more forthcoming with some information.

"You don't think that's likely?" I asked, setting her off again.

"Have you looked at this place? Its over 500 acres. Jordan rode for hours every day, took care of the horses, and the resort. He built all the cabins with his bare hands. He was strong as an ox, and bursting with good health."

I had to agree with most of what she said.

"How was he taking Cam's sudden arrival?"

She shrugged.

"He was going to come back some time. We all knew that."

"Did they get along, though?" I asked.

"Of course they did. They were brothers after all, weren't they?"

"I heard they fought a lot."

"What brothers don't fight? When they were small, they pushed each other in the pond. Now they argued."

"About what?"

"Didn't matter. Whatever Jordan said, Cam had to oppose it. He's always been that way. Loves playing the Devil's Advocate."

"Who, Jordan?"

"Cam! Jordan's the sweet one. Everyone loved him. They all clamored for his attention."

"By all, you mean the people who work for you?"

"Everyone!" Pam enthused. "The ranch hands, the guests who came here, Pa, the locals, the neighbors, they all wanted some attention from Jordan."

"Did he like that?" Tony asked.

Pam shrugged.

"He didn't notice it. He was Mr. Nice Guy. It was all in a day's work for him."

"Did he have any enemies?" I forged ahead.

"Everyone loved him," Pam said, tearing up. "Why would anyone want to harm him?"

I gave her a minute. She plucked off a couple of Kleenex from a side table and blew her nose.

"People never stopped loving him, even after he did."

She had a gleam in her eye. I guessed she had thought of something.

"What do you mean? Are you thinking about someone in particular?"

"His ex," Pam grimaced. "She was a wrong one."

"Were they high school sweethearts? Wasn't that a long time ago?"

I know what they say about a woman scorned. Jordan Harris had been around 27. He must have graduated high school almost eight years ago. Could someone hold a grudge for that long?

"Yes and No. They were in the same high school class and they dated briefly. But nothing happened then. This was more recent. Last year."

I was shocked.

"Er, are you sure? Jessica told me they'd been together since freshman year of college. For 7-8 years."

Pam looked uncomfortable. I waited for her to speak.

"They did meet during freshman year," she began. "They hit it off. They were very much in love and when Jordan graduated, he wanted to get married right away. Jessica wanted to wait until she got her doctorate."

That kind of sounded reasonable.

"Did they fight over it?"

"They had a falling out. Of sorts. Then Jordan ran into this girl from high school. She pursued him. Heavily."

"Wasn't he interested?"

"I think he was confused. He went along with it. They got engaged. She started planning the wedding."

"What happened to Jessica during this time?" Tony asked. "Did she meet Jordan?"

"Maybe once or twice," Pamela replied. "Jordan was very busy at the time. He built the resort from the ground up. He shook up the ranch. Made Pa reduce his hours a bit. He had no time to call his own."

"But he had time to date this girl?" I queried.

"She was here all the time!" Pamela exclaimed. "She lived a mile down the road, so she just walked here when it took her fancy. Or she rode over on her horse."

"Is she a rancher too?" I asked.

"Her! She hasn't done a day's work in her life. Her Pa owned the ranch next door, but he died a few years ago. They let the ranch go to seed after that."

"So Jordan was going to marry this other woman. How did he meet Jessica again?"

I was fascinated by this story. So were Jordan and Jessica destined to be together, or destined to be apart?

"He ran into her at a horse show in Texas," Pam said dreamily. "Her Pa's got a big spread south of the state border."

I nodded. I remembered Jessica telling me that.

"Jordan fell for her again. It was like, they had never been apart."

I sucked in a breath. All this sounded a bit surreal.

"Did they hook up on the spot?" Tony asked suggestively, and I smacked him on his arm.

"They met a few times after that," Pamela said in a hushed voice. "He changed overnight. We could all see it, feel it. He had been dragging his feet as his wedding date drew closer, but he was a changed man once he met Jessica."

"Who did you like more – the ex lady or Jessica?" Tony asked eagerly.

"We just wanted him to be happy. Pa wasn't too happy about him going back on his word. But it was better than repenting at leisure."

"So he broke up with his ex?" I asked.

Pam nodded.

"It was ugly. One minute she was shouting and screaming at him, promising all kinds of vengeance. Then she was gone, like that. She moved away within a week. We never saw her again."

"What happened to her?" I tried to imagine this girl, dumped at the altar, all because of fate.

"Some say they put her in a special place, like a rehab type of thing. We never really knew."

"How did Jessica take it?" Tony wondered.

"I'm not sure what Jordan told her, but she never talked about it. She loved the Triple H. She fit in very well here. Pa took a shine to her, eventually."

I thought about how Jessica had conveniently lied to me about their relationship. She had neglected to mention they were apart for a few years.

"Jessica's very smart. She's working on some special foods that will fatten the cows. You know what that means for a rancher."

Pam sounded wistful. I suspected she had missed her chance at college.

"You're a lot older than the boys, aren't you?" I tipped my head toward the tiny office where we had run into Cam before. I wondered if he was sitting there, listening to us.

"I was a senior in High school when we lost our Ma," she said. "The boys were so young. They needed a guiding hand. Pa was up to his ears in ranch work. So, it all fell to me."

"I lost my mother when I was seven," I shared.

She squeezed my hand, and we shared a moment, tied together in our grief.

Pamela Harris had been more a mother than a sister to the boys. She had given up on college, and maybe a married life of her own. No wonder she looked older than her years.

"They were a joy growing up," Pam's eyes filled up again. "Who would've thought I wouldn't see him grow old."

Tony cleared his throat. I bet he was getting antsy, listening to all this emotional stuff.

"Were you on the ranch that Sunday?" I tried to disguise the question the best way I could. I wanted to know if she was anywhere near Swan Creek.

"Sundays are when my quilting group meets," Pam offered. "There's five or six of us from the county, and one woman a bit more up north."

She named a place that was in between Swan Creek and the Triple H.

"So do you just sit and sew?" Tony feigned interest.

"We have tea and snacks and share patterns and stuff. Mostly we just talk."

"I loved the quilt in our room at the cabin," I praised her. "Did you make that yourself?"

Pamela's face lit up. "I did!" Then she thought back to the day without any more prompting.

"I was feeling queasy that day. I wasn't getting much done. I left around 6."

6 PM. Jordan and Jessica were still having dinner at that time.

"Did you come straight home? Cam said he was out that day too."

"He had a doctor's appointment," Pamela confirmed. "Sunday evenings belong to me. Once I get back to the ranch, it's back to the chores. They never end!"

"So ... you went somewhere else?" I tried to be open.

"I drove around a bit," Pamela said glumly. "Truth be told, I was feeling sorry for myself. For no reason."

She looked apologetic.

"Sometimes I just want to tune all this out, you know. I mean, I love my life, don't get me wrong. And the resort has given me a new lease on it. But some days, you just want to give in to nostalgia."

"I understand," I tried to commiserate.

I suppose I could expect something like that when I reached her age.

She suddenly stood up.

"Where are my manners? How about some coffee?"

I welcomed a hot drink. I wanted to ask many more questions, but I sensed Pam had reached her limit for the day.

Chapter 14

I savored the delicious coffee Pamela served as Tony made small talk with her. I wondered if Cam would put in an appearance. I didn't know if I wanted him to.

"Are you ready to meet Pa?" Pamela asked after I finished my second cup of coffee.

I had devoured a muffin or two while I was at it. The large windows in the lodge provided a dreamy vista. Stark trees with some yellow or brown leaves still clinging to them filled my line of vision. The flurries were still blowing, and they had dusted the ground with a fine white powder by now. I was drowsy but I shook it off. I wondered what Jordan's father would have to say about him.

Pam dropped us off at the main homestead. She begged off to check on the horses.

I knocked on the door and we entered as a gruff voice invited us in. Pa Harris seemed to have aged a bit in the last few days. He was ensconced in an old fashioned wooden rocking chair. He motioned us to a couch beside him. I sat and turned around to face him, craning my neck at the awkward angle.

"Pammie said you are trying to find out what happened to my boy," he rasped.

I gave him a short account of how Sylvie was implicated and how I was trying to clear her name.

"Fair enough. Whatever your reasons, I would be grateful if you find out who harmed my boy."

He gulped, trying to control some emotion.

"You can ask me anything you want. Don't be shy. I will try to answer as much as I can."

I instantly felt better. I was expecting some kind of resistance from the old man.

"Tell me about Jordan," I began.

"Jordan was a smart boy. He went to college, you know. He's the only one in our family who got a fancy college degree."

"Was it of any use on the ranch?" I asked.

What was the use of spending four years at school if you were going to muck stalls for the rest of your life?

"Of course it was. He always knew he would come back and work on the ranch. Even as a kid, he liked making plans for it. He got a degree in agriculture, and in business management."

"Is that where he got the idea of the resort?" I asked.

"The resort was his dream. He created a solid business plan, and built it all from the ground up."

"Pam told us," Tony supplied.

"Does Pamela like living here?" I switched the topic.

The old man frowned.

"What do you mean, little lady? This is her home, ain't it? The only one she's ever known. Now if she had gone and married and lived with her husband, that would be a different deal."

"I know she has to live here. But does she like it?" I pressed.

"I dunno," the old man looked bewildered. "What's that gotta do with my boy Jordan?"

I winced.

"Well, we heard your other boy Cam hates the ranch, so we wondered if Pam hated it too."

"Cam doesn't hate the ranch. He's happy to live here, isn't he? He just loves giving people a hard time."

"So, the Triple H, you named it after your three kids?" Tony leaned forward.

I was glad to have some time to think about my next question.

"These kids?" Pa Harris guffawed. "This ranch has been around for seventy odd years. My grandpa named it after his three sons. My uncles passed away in the wars."

He didn't specify which war, but there had been plenty in the time frame he mentioned.

"My Pa came into it, and he didn't change the name, even though I was an only child. Then when my kids came along, it all made sense again."

"No wonder Jordan wanted to hold on to it," I said.

"Far as I know, all my kids wanted to. If Pammie or Cam are talking about selling the ranch, that's news to me."

"We heard Cam wanted to turn it into an organic farm. Or plant all the acres."

"Pshaw!" the old man flung a hand in the air. "He can talk all he want."

"Were you going to sign the ranch over to Jordan?" I probed.

"I was thinking about it," the old man admitted. "Jordan worked his butt off the last few years. The ranch was bleeding money before that. He deserved it."

"What about your other kids?" I queried. "Didn't they look upon it as their inheritance?"

"I wanted them to work for it," he growled.

"I bet the other two weren't happy about it?"

He shrugged.

"Cam's got his army pension. Pammie – I was sure Jordan would take care of her. Both her brothers would."

"Is the ranch worth a lot?" Tony asked.

"The land must be worth something," the old man nodded. "But the only way to make a living off the ranch is to work it. And that's back breaking work from dawn to dusk. Jordan was doing that. And he was building up the dude ranch business."

"Your sons fought a lot, didn't they?" I questioned.

"Since the day they began to walk," Pa Harris smiled, a faraway look in his eyes. "You'll understand if you have any siblings."

Not a day goes by when Jeet and I don't come to blows. So I got what he was saying.

"Did they hate each other?" Tony asked.

"What kind of damn fool question is that?" the old man roared. "They were family, weren't they?"

I caught Tony's eye and shook my head, signaling him to drop that question.

"Did Jordan have any enemies?"

"And why would he?" the old man demanded. "He turned the ranch around, brought it into the black. He was putting food in the mouths of all the people who work here, and their families. He put a roof over their head."

You would think Jordan Harris was some kind of saint, listening to these people.

"Pam said everyone loved him," I prompted.

"Sure did. They would've done anything for him."

"Do you have any idea who might've wanted to harm him?" I asked.

"I don't. They would be facing the other end of my shotgun if I did."

I decided to ignore that, cringing at the thought of guns stashed somewhere in the old man's living room.

"What about the girl he was supposed to marry?"

"Oh, Jessica! She's a sweet kid. Comes from ranching stock, too."

The old man's face had lit up. He was obviously smitten by Jessica.

"Not her," I said gently. "The other girl Jordan was going to marry."

"Her?" the old man clammed up. "What can I say? I wasn't too happy when Jordan did that. A man's word has to mean something. But then I met Jessica."

"What if Jordan had married that girl? And then run into Jessica? Would he have divorced her to marry Jessica?"

"We'll never know that," the old man said sadly.

Jordan may have been God to these people, but he had definitely wronged this unknown woman in my book.

"You must be quite lonely here, all by yourself?" I went on. "You don't have many neighbors, do you?"

"It's the ranch life. We are used to it." Pa Harris smiled. "I go meet some old fellows at our local pub sometimes. We have a monthly poker game. It's not that bad."

"Were you here on the ranch when Jordan had his date with Jessica?" I wondered if he had somehow wandered into Swan creek too on the fateful day.

"I was right here!" Pa Harris said, and I heaved a sigh of relief.

I hadn't looked forward to treating him like a suspect.

"Must have been a quiet evening, what with Cam and Pamela also out somewhere."

"I was too busy doing Jordan's chores," Pa Harris said. "And then I turned in early, exhausted. Not as strong as I used to be."

He wouldn't have heard either Pamela or Cameron come back that night.

"So you didn't hear Pam or Cameron come in, I suppose?"

He thought a minute, and then shook his head.

"I got up around 11 to get some milk." He looked apologetic. "And some leftover cake. I have a sweet tooth."

I nodded. Raiding the fridge at midnight is something I'm very familiar with.

"I looked out the kitchen window and didn't see Pammie's car. So maybe she wasn't in yet. Although ..."

He stopped, lost in thought.

"She never stays out that late. What was she doing, traipsing about at 11 PM?"

I didn't have an answer for that.

"What about Cam?" Tony nudged.

"I'm not sure about Cam. He parks at the front. He snores the house down. I remember thinking it was pretty quiet."

I was bursting with excitement. Where had Cam and Pamela been that night? I remembered what Pamela had said about Jordan's health.

"Would you say Jordan was in good health?"

"He was strong as an ox. That boy had measles when he was five and other than that, he's never been sick a single day in his life. Never had that flu, even."

I was stumped.

"Any other illnesses in the family? Anything that might cause a sudden death?"

Pa Harris reddened.

"I know what them fool police are saying about my boy. I'm ready to bet the Triple H my boy didn't die of natural causes. He was done in."

He rocked his chair faster as he got irritated. I was beginning to feel dizzy, looking at him. Plus I had a crick in my neck from talking to him at an awkward angle.

"I believe you, Mr. Harris," I tried to calm him down. "That's why I'm trying to find out more."

"So what happens to the ranch now? Is Cam going to build that farm of his?" Tony asked.

Pa Harris looked tired, all of a sudden.

"Don't know! Cam's a big talker but it's hard to say what he's really thinking. Pammie's dedicated, but she needs a guiding hand. She's a woman, after all."

I bristled at this slur to my gender. Tony placed a warning hand on my shoulder.

"Do you think they might have plotted against Jordan?" I asked slowly.

I was expecting some kind of explosive reaction from the old man. A tear rolled down his eye.

"They might have. But they didn't kill him. You write that down, and remember it, little lady. Pammie or Cam didn't harm my boy. Blood's thicker than water."

Tony and I made sympathetic comments. I wondered if I should leave Pa Harris alone in this disturbed state. Pamela solved the problem for me.

"The vet's here for his weekly visit, Pa," Pam called out from the doorway. "He wants to talk to you about that new foal."

The old man nodded and stood up. He shook hands with me and Tony.

"Come back anytime. Help me get justice for my boy."

"Don't worry, Mr. Harris," I said with a confidence that amazed me. "We'll find out what happened. Meanwhile, if you think of something, please call me. Cam has my number."

We walked out and got into Tony's truck. The sun had set while we were talking to Mr. Harris although it was barely 5:30. I was quiet as Tony merged onto the small country road that would take us back home.

"You did good there, sweetie!" Tony answered the question topmost in my mind. "I was proud of you."

"I wasn't too rude, was I? Or abrupt?"

He shook his head. My stomach growled and I wondered if Tony would agree to stop for a snack somewhere.

Chapter 15

I was working reduced hours until a week before Christmas. Then I would be out until the first week of January. We had been so busy working on solving Jordan's death that we had neglected something important.

Pappa put his foot down Sunday morning. We had just finished a lavish breakfast of frittata and skillet potatoes with some peach turnovers Sylvie had sent over. She was used to baking several hours a day. Now she was trying to fill her time, making treats for us in her home kitchen.

"Get ready, kids, we are going out," he said, tapping his cane, his mouth set firmly.

His cheeks were red and they were a sign he was about to blow. Tony and Aunt Reema had come over too.

"What's happening?" Jeet asked, looking sleepy.

"I've left this to you kids for far too long. It's the second week of December!"

"Oops," I clamped a hand on my mouth as I realized the source of Pappa's angst. "Our tree's not up yet."

"It won't be, until we go get one," Pappa roared.

Aunt Reema and Motee Ba giggled. I realized they were in on Pappa's plans. Dad excused himself, citing some deadline.

"Get back here, Anand!" Motee Ba ordered. "You're coming with us."

"But, Ba, the grades are due tomorrow!" Dad protested.

"You can get back to them later."

Dad relented and smiled. We all looked forward to this annual tradition. We piled into the LX and Tony took his truck along. We would need it to haul the trees home. We drove to our favorite tree lot. The sky was overcast and it was dark outside, even though it was morning. The Christmas tree lot was lit up like a stage. Colorful lights were strung on trees. Christmas music played from speakers.

Many people must have had the same thoughts as us, judging by the crowds. A man signaled us and we followed him.

"I've set aside these two firs for you. Both are about 6 feet."

We stared at two beautiful trees hung with a SOLD sign.

"Thanks Bud," Dad clapped him on the back.

"We want to look around some," I said, and went deeper into the lot.

I ran into the Robinsons, Nancy and Nellie. They were trying to pick out a tree.

"Hello," I said cheerfully. "Looking forward to your first Christmas in Swan Creek?"

Nancy's lip curled.

"You bet. We already got two trees for the restaurant. We hired a decorator from the city to do them. People are loving them trees."

I promised I would come and look at them.

"We are worked off our feet, you know," Nellie gleamed. "What with being the only restaurant in town. I finally had to drag Ma here to get a tree for home."

"So your business is doing good, then?" I asked unnecessarily.

I was quite aware of what they had done to make it so.

Nellie's head bobbed up and down in excitement.

"And you didn't want to move here," she said to her mother. "I told you I would make it right. Didn't I, Ma?"

Nancy looked uncomfortable.

"Are you from around here? What made you pick Swan Creek for your diner?" I asked curiously.

"We are from down south," Nancy tried to brush me off.

"Isn't the diner business better?" Nellie squealed.

Nancy shushed her and dragged her away, frowning at me. I wondered what I had done wrong.

We loaded our trees in the back of Tony's truck and went home. Jeet was sent up into the attic to fetch the boxes of Christmas decorations. Many of these were handmade, from crafts projects at school, or stuff Motee Ba had taught me to make. There was a crochet angel my Mom had knitted when she was pregnant with Jeet.

We had fun putting the tree up. Lunch was ordered in, and we were finally ready to light the tree that evening. Everyone clapped as Pappa settled into his chair. He had enjoyed the day, tapping his cane, ordering everyone about.

I went into the guest house and started working on my program. I was close to finishing it. I had made no progress over the binder. I forced myself to bring some kind of order to all the information. I started a spreadsheet and began listing out all the organizations that had been contacted, and all the police departments that had sent over some report, or worked on Mom's case. Slowly, something began to take shape.

I realized the last inquiry about Mom had been made 15 years ago. My first order of business was going to be putting in a fresh inquiry. I needed them to make her file active.

Another thing I realized was that only the neighboring states had been contacted. This included Texas to the South, Arkansas to the East and New Mexico to the West. Kansas and Colorado had been added later.

I thought about spreading a wider net. What if Mom got on a bus that was going to Florida? The possibilities were endless, but I was determined.

I was not going to leave out any option that came to mind.

I fell into a dreamless sleep, tired out from all the physical labor.

I was munching my cereal the next morning when I remembered something. I talked to Tony on my way to work.

He rung up my usual coffee and threw in a candy bar.

"You must be looking forward to a slower day at work."

I bobbed my head. "You have no idea. Hopefully, I can just doze at my desk. How about lunch?"

"I'll pick you up."

I walked out of the library at 11:40. Tony's truck was parked in a spot close to Park Street. Most campus spots were empty and now that there were no classes, the campus cops were being a bit lenient.

I got in and directed him toward the highway.

"Are you going to cook something at home?" Tony asked.

I shook my head.

"It's been a while since we checked out the competition."

"Oh!" he nodded and smiled.

Nancy's parking lot was packed as expected. Tony did the smart thing and parked in Sylvie's lot. We crossed the street over to Nancy's Fancy Diner. Now that Jon and Sylvie's place was sealed, all the locals went to Nancy's. There weren't too many options in a town like Swan Creek.

There was a 15 minute wait and we sat on the curb, enjoying the winter sunshine. I told Tony about the spreadsheet I had started.

"Let's divvy it up. We can work on a script and then we'll say the same thing to every department we call. Don't try to do it all yourself, Meera!"

The hostess beckoned and we went in. I spotted many familiar faces. Some were older people from town, some were people I knew on campus. Office workers, professors, Bingo playing grandmas – they had all converged at Nancy's. I supposed I couldn't really blame them. People have to eat, after all.

A few people waved at us, and a few tried to dodge us, looking uncomfortable. I made it a point to call out to them and say Hello.

Nancy's was on a roll. They offered Early Bird Specials for seniors. They had bottomless coffee for people who spent more than $10. They had Lunch Specials under $5. Whoever was doing this had a great business mind. I had to admit Sylvie had never thought of these things.

"Do you want the soup and sandwich special?" a young waitress in a spiffy uniform asked us.

Her sunny yellow dress matched the color the building had been painted.

"What kind of soup?" Tony asked.

The waitress pointed to a placard on the table. There were three types of soups and three types of sandwich. If you went for the special, you could choose any soup from the list, and any sandwich. You got a cup of soup and half a sandwich.

I chose the tomato soup and the chicken salad sandwich. Tony went for the French Onion soup with roast beef. Our meal appeared almost instantly. They must have the soup ladled out in bowls, ready to go.

The food was okay, but portion sizes were small. Dessert was called for.

"I don't suppose you have pie," Tony began, ready to give the girl a hard time about it.

"Apple, cherry or pecan," she quipped.

"You're serving pie?" we both burst out. "I thought you people were against pie."

The waitress shrugged. She looked harried and I decided to give her a break. We put in our order and also asked for a coffee refill. Since our check was more than 10 bucks, I suppose we qualified for the bottomless cup.

Our pies came and I plunged a fork in, not expecting much. My eyes popped as I tasted the pie. Tony was having the same reaction.

"I bet you 50 bucks this is Sylvie's pie!" I cried.

A few people turned around. Most people knew who Sylvie was. They looked interested.

"Who made this pie, hunh?" I scowled at the waitress.

"It's artisanal," she said with a straight face.

"You bet it's artisanal. You put this artisan out of business. And now you're peddling the same pie in your diner? How dare you?"

My hunch was proven. I had wondered where Sylvie was sending off all those pies. Nancy's had been the most obvious, considering there weren't too many restaurant type establishments in Swan Creek.

Nancy and Nellie came rushing out. Nancy breathed fire. Nellie looked scared.

"What's the problem here?"

She spotted us and folded her arms.

"You! What are you doing here?"

"Having lunch! Just like everyone else. And what do I see? You're serving Sylvie's pie. After you put her out of business."

"What are you implying, hunh? Stay out of my bidness."

Nancy was angry but she also looked guilty.

"So you agree Sylvie made this pie?" I asked.

"We source a lot of our items from artisanal suppliers. We don't give out their names. We have exclusive contracts with them."

I wonder how Nancy came up with all this mumbo jumbo.

"You should be ashamed!" I felt a vein throb in my neck.

I curled my fists, afraid I was about to dock her one. Tony put a warning hand on my arm.

"I'm running an honest business here. The artisans supply a product and I pay for it. It's a simple business transaction between two people. What is your problem?"

"That's just a lot of crap!" I snorted.

I looked around. Almost every person in Nancy's was staring at us.

"And you! Y'all should be ashamed too. Sylvie's fed you for thirty years. And you're consorting with the enemy at the first sign of trouble."

A part of me realized I was losing it. I had just accused a roomful of people of something. I just wasn't sure what.

A woman hissed at her companion.

"Didn't I tell you this tasted familiar?"

"I can spot Sylvie's pie from a mile," an oldie with a cane said with a toothless grin.

"Is it true?" A man in a suit asked Nancy.

I think he was one of the big wigs at the graduate college at Pioneer.

"Did you put Sylvie out of business?"

Nancy squirmed, and denied it.

The crowd suddenly got bolder and began to fling questions at the mother-daughter duo. Nellie was sweating like a pig, her hair in disarray. Nancy was calmly fielding all the questions, but her ears were red, the only sign of any discomfort.

Tony tugged at me and motioned toward the door. The waitress came and slapped a bill down at our desk.

"Why have you charged us for a refill?" I demanded, spotting the double charge for coffee. "Our check is above 10 bucks."

"That's 10 bucks per person," she said glibly.

Tony slapped a 20 on the table.

"Don't keep the change!"

The girl came back with the change and we stepped out. Nancy was still dealing with the commotion but I felt her razor sharp glare on my back.

Was I going to be sorry I messed with her?

We crossed the road and I collapsed on a bench on Sylvie's porch.

"You already knew they were serving Sylvie's pies, didn't you?" Tony's eyes crinkled.

"I guessed, but I wanted to be sure. Why do you think Sylvie's dealing with them? Are things that bad?"

Tony looked uncomfortable.

"Maybe they are. It's not something we should ask them about though, Meera. Maybe Granny's a better person for it."

I nodded.

Tony drove me back to the library.

"See you in a couple of hours."

I waved goodbye to Tony and went in.

Chapter 16

We had decided to meet and discuss what we had found out about Jordan. Becky, Tony and I were already present at the guest house. Stan Miller was supposed to come by. I was looking forward to getting some more information from him, however much he was willing to disclose.

I had set out some munchies. Brainstorming is hungry work at the best of times. My black bean dip was hearty enough to stick to tortilla chips. I had arranged the dip, fresh guacamole and chipotle sour cream in small bowls. A large bowl was overflowing with tortilla chips. There were some buffalo chicken bites for a more hearty option.

"Do we have to wait for Stan?" Becky grumbled.

"I'm here," he called out from the door.

He took off his cap and placed it on a side table. I let him have a few sips of his soda and a few bites. Then I began.

"It's like this. We've met a few people over the last couple of weeks. There's a lot of information. I just want to pool it and try to make sense out of it."

I had set up a white board in one corner. Being a professor's abode, there is no lack of teaching aids in our house. I'm also a very visual person. Charts and lists are my weapon in solving any problem.

Becky picked up a marker. We decided to create small sub headings as we went along.

"So, people we have talked to …' I began and Becky started a section for people who had already been interviewed.

"Jessica, Pamela, Pa Harris and Cameron," I called out.

Stan looked impressed.

"You managed to meet them all? We've had a hard time making

the old man talk."

"Jordan Harris was intelligent. He got a degree at Pioneer, and built a dude ranch from the ground up. According to his Pa, he turned the ranch around, so he was smart."

Stan nodded. Tony and Becky already knew this.

"Most people loved him. Or rather, no one hated him. Cam, Pamela, Pa Harris and Jessica have all said that. Except, he dumped a girl at the altar. And what do you bet this girl bore a grudge?"

"Who's this girl?" Stan wanted to know.

"No one mentioned her name and I didn't ask."

I mentally cursed myself for this slip.

I stood up and started an Action Items section. 'Find more about' ex went under it.

"Cameron is an unstable character," Tony stated next. "Pamela thought he wanted to start a farm on the ranch or something. He told us he wanted to start a convalescent home for veterans. Pa Harris said Cam was just bluffing."

"I think he was just sounding Jordan out. He wanted to know if he was welcome at the ranch."

"Why wouldn't he be?" Stan asked, scooping up some guacamole with a tortilla chip.

"He never liked the ranch. He went away and joined the Army. Came back recently facing a discharge. Jordan did most of the work to make the ranch profitable. He may not have wanted his brother to just come and enjoy the fruits of his labor."

"If that's true, Jordan was the goose laying the golden egg," Stan pointed out. "Why would Cam want to harm him?"

I conceded the point.

"Wait a minute. Didn't the siblings say the old man was going to sign over the ranch to Jordan? Maybe they wanted their inheritance."

"In that case, it made sense to bump the old man off," Becky said. "Pamela and Cam would get their share, and Jordan would still do all the work."

"Don't forget they fought a lot," Tony reminded me.

"I don't think that means anything," I protested. "Jeet and I are at each other's throats almost every day. But I'd lay down my life for him."

"You're forgetting one thing," Stan said complacently. "Jordan Harris died here in Swan Creek. That ranch of theirs is about 60 miles away. None of the family were in the vicinity."

"But that's just it," I cried. "They could have been in Swan Creek. Cam admitted being in the city until 8 PM. He could have driven by here. Pamela wasn't home either. She said she was just driving around, she doesn't know where. And Pa Harris said neither of them was in bed at 11 PM."

Stan leaned forward, looking dumbfounded.

"What are you saying, Meera? That's news to me."

He made a note in a small notebook.

"Don't say anything to them about this now," he warned. "Now that we know they weren't home, we can ask them for alibis. And we can ask them exactly where they were. They are obligated to answer. They may not show you the same courtesy."

I wasn't sure about that but I let it slide.

"What about Jessica?" I asked Stan. "She said she talked to him at 10. That means he was alive at that time."

Stan looked shocked again.

"She said what? She never told us that."

"Do you think she lied?" Tony asked.

"What is the estimated time of death?" I asked Stan.

"Between 9 and midnight. They can't narrow it down more than that. And it's possible he was incapacitated even before that. So he could've been on that bench but unconscious."

"Jessica's call is really important, in that case," I nodded.

"What if someone else answered Jordan's phone? She should be able to tell the difference, right?" Becky came up with a bizarre question.

I was stunned.

"Have we made any progress at all?" I wrung my hands.

"Plenty!" Stan said, getting up. "Thanks to you, we know the brother is flaky. There could be an ex. Jessica may or may not be lying."

"She lied about being engaged."

I told Stan how she had let me believe she and Jordan had been together for 7 years.

"So she lied outright," Stan mused. "Maybe she was hurt the first time they broke up, and she was just stringing him along this time? Waiting for the right opportunity to have her revenge?"

"That's cold blooded," I winced.

"If Jordan didn't die naturally, chances are he ingested some kind of toxin or poison. Who could have had access to that?"

"All his family insisted he was very healthy and strong as an ox," I repeated. "He was only 27, after all."

"Jessica works on some kind of wonder food for cows, doesn't she?" Tony asked.

I remembered and explained it to Stan.

"What does that entail, exactly? Maybe she deals with poisons every day. Maybe what's super food for a cow is harmful to humans?" Tony was seriously considering Jessica as a suspect.

I added another line to the Action Items list – find out who had access to poison.

"We are nowhere close to solving this, are we?" I was frustrated. "Jon and Sylvie's have been closed for over a week."

"You have to be patient, Meera!" Stan consoled us. "I think you have done a pretty good job for amateurs. Let's catch up again in a week or so."

Stan stood up and scooped up one more tortilla chip. He adjusted his cap on his head and turned to leave.

"One moment Meera."

He looked uncomfortable.

"That woman was spotted on campus again. Near the library. One of the school cops called it in. She was gone by the time we got there."

I flung my hands up in the air.

"This woman's like the bogey man. What's her interest in me? Does she really want to harm me?"

"If I had to guess, I'd say No," Stan said soothingly. "She's had plenty of chances to accost you. She hasn't made any contact yet. Maybe she's just senile, or a bit touched. Maybe you remind her of someone and she wants to look at you."

"I'm not going to worry about her," I said stoutly.

Truth be told, I was finally beginning to worry. I tried to focus on the matter at hand.

"We need to find out more about Jordan's ex. And maybe talk to someone who knows Jessica."

"What about her lab mates?" Tony asked. "Shouldn't we confirm she actually turned up for that meeting that night? Or that she was in the lab later on?"

I added two more items to the Action Items list.

We talked about various alternate scenarios, and tried to come up with a motive. Did someone hate Jordan enough to kill him? Or was it all just about money?

"That's it. I've had enough. Let's do something else."

Everyone was hungry, inspite of having grazed on the tortilla chips.

I pulled a platter of marinated chicken from the refrigerator. Tony fired up the grill. I lined some corn on the cob on one side. The chicken had absorbed all the adobo seasoning and tequila I had doused it in earlier. I placed the boneless pieces on the grill and called the main house.

"We're grilling some chicken, Motee Ba," I told her. "Are you guys ready to eat?"

Jeet was the first to come over. Pappa followed, tapping his cane. Motee Ba held a rice cooker in her hand.

"I made some rice pilaf," she called out. "I think it will go well with the chicken."

I put a plate aside for Dad, knowing he would probably be busy.

We sat on the patio, warmed by a fire Tony had built.

"Your aunt may be coming for a visit," Motee Ba announced.

"Oh, cool!" I tried to be stoic.

My aunt is a trial at the best of times. She would come armed with photos of eligible Indian boys and follow me around, extolling their virtues. She would not be pleased about what I was involved in.

I met Tony for lunch at the food court the next day. The Wok was the only place open so we got stir frys.

"Granny called me. There's a message for you from your blue eyed boy."

"What does he want now?" I asked Tony, ignoring his sarcasm.

"Why don't you call him back?" Tony shrugged his shoulders.

I borrowed Tony's cell phone and put in a call to Cam.

"Hello Meera! Got a minute?" he asked cheerfully.

"Sure. You called?"

"I have an appointment in the City today. I'll be going back around 6. Would you like to have dinner with me?"

I was amazed. Was Cam asking me out on a date? Then I remembered I needed to ferret out lots of information from him. A dinner date would be a good opportunity.

"Why not? Did you have a place in mind?"

"I don't know much about Swan Creek. Just tell me where to be, and at what time."

I picked a pub I liked, counting on it being crowded even on a weekday evening. We planned to meet at 6:30.

"Will you be safe?" Tony asked as I hung up.

"Relax! That's why I chose Jimmy's. What's he gonna do in a roomful of people?"

Dinner time arrived soon enough and I waited for Cam at Jimmy's, a local bar.

He came in, looking pleased.

"I lost the cane," he announced, turning in a circle.

"Congratulations!" I was genuinely happy for him.

"We are celebrating. Dinner's on me."

He signaled the server and ordered a large beer and a platter of appetizers.

"What will you have?" he raised his eyebrows and looked at me.

"A Coke," I told the server.

"Is that all?" Cam protested. "How about something stronger?"

"Maybe later," I smiled.

He poured out the details about his doctor's appointment.

"Are you done with your therapy then?"

"No. Therapy's even more important now. I need to build my strength. Luckily, I have access to the best equine therapy in the state."

"Aren't these the same horses you hated?" I teased.

"You're right," he sobered. "Life comes full circle, hunh!"

The appetizers arrived and I gave them the attention they deserved. You have to respect the fried platter at Jimmy's or he'll give you the evil eye.

"Have you thought any more about what you'll do now?" I asked after he downed his second beer.

"I have to talk to Pam," he said. "Pa's never really asked her what she wanted. She's just a woman, according to him."

"She's great at handling the guests. And she seems to love the resort."

Cam lapsed into thought.

"Were you serious about the farm? Or the convalescent home? Or going to live in Dallas?" I let him know I was on to him.

Cam was apologetic.

"Ok. You got me. But I was only half kidding."

"Your Pa says you love to rile people up."

He flashed me a devilish grin. The blue of his irises deepened and his whole face creased in a smile.

"I've been accused of that before, but I wasn't lying outright."

"Oh?" I challenged.

"I do want to turn at least part of the resort into a special home for veterans. The equine therapy will be a big draw. So will the organic farm. We do grow our own vegetables now. Maybe we'll do it on a larger scale as we add more cabins. And the Dallas part? I've put some feelers out. I want to be a speaker on the Army circuit. Give motivational talks, that kind of thing."

He paused and drained his glass again.

I was impressed. The Jordan family wasn't lacking in smarts.

"All those plans depend on having access to the ranch though, right?"

Cam sobered.

"And you think I would kill my brother for that piece of land?"

I was quiet.

He leaned forward.

"Jordan was willing to hand the Triple H over to me. He told me that himself."

"How? When?" I asked. "And wouldn't he have to own the ranch to be able to do that?"

"Actually, I'm the sole heir to the Triple H according to my grandpa's will."

"But I thought your Pa was going to hand it over to Jordan."

"Yes, he was," Cam said bitterly. "He always considered Jordan to be the true heir."

"So he wouldn't actually be giving it away. You'd still own it?"

I was trying to keep track.

"On paper, yes. But what does a piece of paper matter? Jordan was the one Pa chose."

I was confused. This totally ruled out money as a motive.

"So you're saying all this talk of what each of you wanted means nothing? You'll own the ranch no matter what?"

"That's right, beautiful. The ranch is not the prize. It never was. Winning Pa's approval is."

"And now you'll never know," I said under my breath.

Cam clinked his glass with mine and gave me a thumbs up sign.

"Got that right."

I motioned to the server to bring some coffee.

"Are you sure you are okay to drive back to the ranch tonight?" I was concerned about the five beers he had guzzled in an hour.

"Don't worry," Cam held up a hand. "I can sleep it off at Jessica's. She's probably in that lab of hers anyway."

Chapter 17

My dinner with Cam – I didn't want to call it a date – had shaken me up. If the Triple H was really coming to him, it ruled out money as a motive. I couldn't shake off how casual he had sounded about staying over at Jessica's. I had a feeling he had done it before. Was he trying to steal her away from Jordan? Had the brothers fought over a girl?

Tony and I stood outside his gas station, sipping large cups of scalding hot coffee. The mid December morning was cold and bracing and I was waiting for the caffeine to kick in and jolt me awake.

"This just gets more complicated each day," Tony complained. "Any news of how the diner inspection is progressing?"

I shook my head.

"They're short staffed. With the holidays, they might not get to it until the next year."

"How's Sylvie taking it? I hope you're not giving her grief about supplying pies to Nancy's."

"Of course I'm not!"

Sometimes Tony has zero faith in me.

Something about Sylvie supplying pies to Nancy's didn't sit right with me. I thought about it but nothing obvious came to mind. Then I let it go. It was Sylvie's call, after all.

"I'm meeting Pamela at the ranch later today. How about coming with us?"

"Is Becky going?" Tony asked.

I nodded.

"In that case, I'll pull out this time. I have some inventory to catch up on."

I put in a few hours at work and was ready to drive to the Triple H. Becky and I picked up some tacos from a drive through, with a double order of locos. I steered the car with one hand, giving my taco the attention it deserved. The country roads were almost deserted but it was slow going because of the icy patches.

"What are you planning to ask her today, Meera?"

"I want to ask her where she was that day, but she might take offense and chuck us out."

"What about Jordan's ex?"

"That too," I nodded.

"Let's lead with that," Becky suggested, "and then ask about her alibi."

I pulled up outside the Lodge and went in. Pam was waiting for us at the small seating area next to the tall windows. She motioned us over with a nod and we joined her.

"I hope you're a cautious driver. These roads can get icy."

She poured coffee for everyone and we settled down.

"Have you made any progress?" she asked.

I was noncommittal.

"We're just trying to get as much background information as we can. For example, we know nothing about this woman Jordan dated for a while."

"Oh, Eleanor? What's to know about her? She was batty. They finally put her in an asylum."

"Is she still there?" Becky asked.

"I don't know," Pam said. "I suppose they would let us know if they released her?"

"And why would they do that?" I quizzed her.

"She attacked Jordan, didn't she? Almost gauged his eyes out.

She agreed to go to that mental place instead of jail. Only because the local magistrate was a friend of her Pa's."

"How is it you didn't mention this to the police?" I demanded.

Pam looked bewildered.

"I never thought of it. Once Jessica came back into Jordan's life, he was so happy. And we were all happy for them. I hadn't thought of this girl in a while."

I gave her Stan's number.

"He's one of the people working on Jordan's case. I think you should tell him everything. They can check and tell us where she is right now."

Pam took the note, looking disturbed.

"You think this is important, don't you?"

"It's best to consider all possible scenarios," I tried to soothe her. "Have you remembered where you were driving around on Sunday night?"

"Why don't you ask me directly if I was in Swan Creek?" she demanded.

"I'm just trying to help."

Pam stood up, clearly signaling our meeting was done. She walked over to the check-in desk and handed me an envelope.

"Your refund. I'm sorry your visit was cut short. And now you're helping us find who harmed Jordan."

I took the envelope from her. It would come in handy in my Christmas shopping.

"How's your Pa?" I asked politely. "Please tell him I stopped by."

"You can do that yourself."

Pam's temper had cooled down a bit. She drove us to the

homestead in her golf cart. Pa Harris was in the barn, rubbing down a horse.

"Hello, little lady."

His face crinkled in a smile.

We made some small talk and I fed an apple to the horse. Pam offered to drive us back to my car but we chose to walk. Becky and I huddled in our jackets, shivering but enjoying the cold. We walked faster to work up some warmth. I almost crashed into a body.

"Watch where you're going," a friendly voice called out.

I slipped the hood of my jacket down. Cam was bundled up just like us. He held a large straw basket in his arms, filled with all kinds of vegetables. His hands were muddy. He held them out.

"Sorry I can't shake hands."

"Are those your organic vegetables?" I peered at the basket with interest.

"Kale, turnips, sweet potatoes … what's that?" I pointed to some greens.

"Chard, and winter squash. And mushrooms, of course."

"Are these wild mushrooms?" Becky asked.

"Some of them are," Cam nodded. "But you've got to be careful. They taste great in soups and sauces, but they can be deadly."

Becky's eyes were as big as saucers.

I pulled her along and said goodbye to Cam. I kept a tight hold on Becky's arm, hoping she wouldn't blurt out anything until we got inside the car.

"Did you see that?" Becky asked. "Do you think …"

I shook my head. So Cam had access to poisonous mushrooms. At least he knew how to tell them apart. I had to report this to Stan right away.

"Maybe they already tested for mushrooms," I said lamely.

We were quiet as I drove under the arches of the Triple H and merged onto the country road that would take us home. We passed the sign for the country store we had stopped at earlier. I pulled into their lot on a hunch.

The hostess recognized us from our previous visit.

"Pot pies are just coming out," she beamed.

My mouth watered at the thought of buttery pastry and creamy sauce with juicy chunks of meat. Becky and I both nodded eagerly.

I put my head down and worked on my pie. I can be quite devoted that way.

Becky kicked me under the table.

"Meera," she whispered, tipping her head to one side.

I looked around. The place was empty except for a table in the corner. A lone figure wearing a long winter coat sat huddled, sipping a cup of coffee. It was hard to say if it was a man or woman from the angle.

"That woman ..." Becky whispered. "I think she was in the drive through line at the taco place."

"So?" I rolled my eyes.

Becky gave me a meaningful glare. I snapped out of the pie induced stupor and turned around swiftly. Becky kicked me again. We pretended to be busy eating. The figure stood up and went out without giving us a second glance.

"See? That person didn't even give us a glance."

"I don't know, Meera," Becky was glum.

The woman came by to clear our plates.

"You want to know something funny?" she asked. "Old lady over there was here the last time you had lunch. We see very few people out here in the backwoods, and then the same people turn up twice, at the same time!"

She walked away, shaking her head.

I placed some cash on the table as the woman handed over the check.

"Have you had this store for long?"

"My family's been here for over a hundred years," the woman smiled. "My Ma started this country store and restaurant. I was her only child, so I settled down here with my family."

"You must know people from the surrounding areas, then?"

"That I do. It's a shame what happened to that Harris boy. But I say he had it coming."

"We heard he was very well loved."

I looked at her face.

"By most folks, yes."

Her face had set in a frown. Becky cut to the chase.

"Are you talking about the girl he jilted? We heard she was insane."

"She was nothing of that sort. I bounced her on my knee when she was a baby. She was such a sweet girl. Then that Harris boy went and fell for some girl at that fancy college of his. He couldn't dump our local girl quick enough."

"She took it hard?" I prodded.

"That she did. Mother and daughter both moved away."

"Really, where?" I asked urgently.

"No one knows. Now, how about some dessert?"

We shook our heads and thanked the lady. I rushed home as fast as I could. The first call I put in was for Stan.

"I say, Meera, you should join the police force. That's a lot of information to process."

I hung up, feeling pleased with myself. I called Tony next and told him everything that had happened.

"Slow down, Meera! So Pam won't tell us her alibi, Cam had access to poisonous mushrooms, Jordan's ex attacked him once … Is that all?"

I had to tell him about the woman. I could hear him almost fall out of bed.

"Do you believe me now?" he roared.

"We don't know it's the same woman. Looked like some dowdy old lady. Maybe she just stopped there for a snack like we did."

"Yeah, right!" Tony refused to believe me.

I hung up. I didn't want to listen to his tirade. I walked into the kitchen, sniffing at what was cooking.

"Hungry?" Motee Ba asked.

"Not really," I said. "What's for dinner?"

"*Khichdi*," Motee Ba smiled, knowing I wouldn't refuse.

This lentil and rice stew is a staple in any Patel household. Warm, mushy, topped with plenty of ghee with a side of fried *papads*, this is the comfort food on which I was raised.

My image processing program was almost ready to be tested. I was eager to find out how successful I was in the first round. I would need to tweak it but I was hoping I wasn't too far off mark.

I checked the special email I had set up for Mom's case. Some of the departments I had approached had responded. Some needed paperwork to make Mom's case active. Some had already done it. Most of them wanted a photograph. I sent out my specially drafted email to 10 more people in Arizona and Alabama. I was widening the net bit by bit, sending the email to a new set of departments every day. I had a long list to get through.

That night, I dreamed I was flying down an icy road. I yanked the steering with my hands but it didn't respond. A car followed me, a hooded figure at the wheel. Sleet came in through the windows, soaking me. I braked hard and the car skidded, going round in circles on the narrow road.

I woke with a start. My bedroom window was open, the flimsy sheers soaked from the rain coming in. I rushed to the window, pulling it close, trying to shut it against the icy wind and sleet. Just as the window snapped close, I spied a silhouette by the guest house. I broke out in a cold sweat, refusing to believe it.

I was just remembering the figure from my dream, wasn't I?

Chapter 18

I had a tough time getting out of my bed Monday morning. It was my last day at work and I just had to put in a few hours before the school closed for the rest of the year. I tried to clear my foggy brain as I sat in bed, unwilling to climb out of the covers.

Someone rapped loudly on my door.

"7:30!" Motee Ba called out.

I slurped the warm oatmeal she had made and got dressed.

"I had a bad dream," I told Tony when I stopped to talk to him on my way to work. "It's got me unsettled."

"Eat this," he handed me a candy bar, smiling.

I was so disturbed I said no to candy.

I manned the library desk and chatted with one or two lone wolves who were stocking up on books for the 2 week break. These were the incorrigible geeks, or kids doing some research on a deadline. Soon as I thought of research, I thought of a better way to utilize my time.

I bundled up and walked over to the Chemical Engineering building. The girl from earlier greeted me. She was wearing a red sweater with a holiday motif. She remembered me.

"Hello. You again?"

"Can you tell me where Jessica's lab is?"

"Her research group has an office in the bio technology building. That's where their lab is."

"Oh, thanks. I thought she's in your department."

"She is," the girl nodded. "Her research is cross disciplinary. Their team's made up of people from different departments."

"Gotcha," I thanked the girl and turned to go.

"Have some cake. It's our annual end of year cake. It's good!"

She pointed to a large sheet cake placed on a side table. It had been sampled generously but a good part of it was still remaining. Tiny red plates and forks were placed next to it.

"Thanks. I will."

I beamed at her. Life's too short to say no to free cake.

I cut myself a generous slice and waved good bye. I went outside and chose a spot where I could lean against the wall comfortably. I made short work of the cake, and made my way to the bio technology lab. I was freezing by the time I pulled open the heavy glass doors that flanked the department.

I walked down a flight of stairs and stood outside a door that listed Jessica's name along with a few others.

"Come on in," a voice hollered from inside in answer to my knock.

Three or four workstations lined the wall. There was a desk in the center with some fancy equipment I couldn't make much sense of.

"Er, I'm looking for Jessica," I explained.

It was obvious she wasn't there.

A moon faced man with spectacles ogled me.

"She should be here soon. What is it about?"

The man was shorter than me, and he had a rumpled look about him. If I had to guess, I'd say he had probably spent the night huddled over the computer. Yellow rings of sweat circled his underarms and a faint odor I didn't want to think about wafted my way. He was almost bald, and he was licking his lips every few seconds. But he wasn't that much older than me.

"It's sort of personal," I hedged.

"I'm Colin Stevens," he said, standing up, offering me a hand.

I shook it reluctantly. This guy gave me an unclean feeling.

"Meera Patel."

"You're welcome to wait here," he offered.

I nodded and decided to take him up on the offer.

He went back to the papers he was reading and there was a deathly silence in the room for about five minutes. He kept licking his lips all the time, reminding me of a repulsive reptile.

"Not much I don't know about Jessica, you know." He crossed his fingers and held up his hand. "We are like this!"

"She hasn't mentioned you." I feigned surprise. "But I guess that's understandable. She's going through a rough time."

It was Colin's turn to act surprised.

"Really? Why is that?"

"Haven't you heard?" I leaned forward. "Her fiancée was found dead by the lake."

Colin Stevens didn't bat an eyelid.

"Are you talking about Jordan? They were breaking up."

I hid my shock well.

"No. they were celebrating their engagement."

"That's what they told everyone! To get away from that ranch and meet somewhere they could talk in private."

The slimy snake had a triumphant look on his face.

I cleared my throat.

"And why were they breaking up?"

Colin beamed from ear to ear.

"She's with me now, of course. We've been dating a while. Ever since we started working together on this project."

"When was that?" I asked.

"About three years ago."

I was finding this hard to process. I tried a different tack.

"Are you also a chemical engineer?"

"No. I'm a doctor." Colin puffed up again. "A veterinary doctor, of course."

"I don't really know what Jessica's research is about," I admitted.

"This is a cross disciplinary group," Colin Stevens explained. "We have programmers and statistics experts. Then we have people doing simulations. Jessica and I do most of the field work."

"Like what?" I had to ask.

"Working with the heifers… injecting our test subjects with different serums, taking blood and tissue samples, evaluating and mapping their progress… Stuff like that."

"Sounds very different from chemical engineering."

Colin Stevens shrugged.

"Jessica's great at it. She grew up on a cattle ranch."

This I did know.

"Real life applications of science require a lot of knowhow from different fields. Very different from academia." Colin Stevens said pompously. "We are one of the most advanced research teams on campus."

"I heard Jessica's graduating soon."

"We need her here. She got side tracked a bit with all that Jordan Harris business. This is where her true calling is."

"So she's not graduating then?" I prompted.

"I'm the Head Researcher on the project," Colin Stevens stood up, towering over me. "I might sign off on her PHD once she decides to stay on here."

"And has she?" I asked.

"She will. She has no more distractions with Jordan out of the way."

I was bursting with this unexpected bounty of information. Was this guy above board, or was he lying?

"So you're happy Jordan's dead?" I asked bluntly.

Colin Stevens finally began looking flustered.

"That's not what I meant."

I was quiet, hoping he would spill more. And he did.

"It's just…it's hard, watching Jessica fawn over these pups of hers. But she always comes back to me. I'm a patient man, Ms. Patel."

"You're saying Jessica's a tease?" I didn't mince words.

"Not my choice of words, but yeah, something like that. I don't blame her. A beauty like her is bound to slay hearts."

The basement room was beginning to close in on me.

The door flung open with a rush and Jessica came in, followed by a couple of other guys.

"We're here," she called out cheerfully and stopped when she saw me.

"Hi Meera!"

"Hey Jessica!" I greeted her back. "I just came back to see how you were doing?"

Colin Stevens interrupted.

"You're 5 minutes late, guys. We need to start our meeting."

I was being booted out.

"Let's catch up later," Jessica pleaded.

I stood up and clambered up the stairs, rushing out to get some fresh air. I couldn't get out of there fast enough.

An hour ago, we hadn't even known Colin Stevens existed. Now he had provided a boatload of new information. I wanted to think he was some kind of psycho, spouting off delusions about Jessica. But I couldn't ignore what he had said without checking it out.

I walked back to my desk and sat out the remaining hour, clearing up as much as I could. Finally, it was time to leave and I rushed out, driving to Tony's gas station. Two weeks of holidays lay ahead, and I couldn't suppress the smile that broke out on my face.

"Hey Babe!" Tony high fived me as I got out of my car. "Are we celebrating?"

"Of course! I'm starving, and I have quite the scoop for you guys. Where's Becky?"

We debated over going out for lunch or rustling something up at home. We chose to go home. Becky was waiting for us at the guest house, busy making lunch.

"Enchiladas!" she pointed to the oven.

The day stretched before us, and the bubbly, cheesy, casserole was perfect for the cold weather.

We loaded our plates with two enchiladas each, a side of refried beans and rice. I took double helpings of sour cream and guacamole.

We attacked the food and no one spoke for the first 2- 3 bites. Okay, maybe 10 bites.

"What's this scoop you were talking about?" Tony asked.

I narrated my encounter with Colin Stevens. Tony and Becky

were struck dumb. Their eyes popped and I sat back, feeling smug.

"Is that a new development, or what?"

"Has Jessica verified any of this?" Becky asked with a frown. "Maybe this guy's just bad mouthing her."

"I didn't get a chance to talk to her. But I'm thinking, of course she'll deny all this, won't she? Even if it's true."

"Don't see her admitting she was two timing Jordan," Tony agreed.

We finished our meal and collapsed in front of the TV. Becky and I each took one end of the couch, and Tony staked claim to a deep chair. A few flurries started, and I remembered my dream.

Tony laughed out loud.

"You think I was dreaming?" I demanded.

"I don't know Meera, but now you know how I feel when you dismiss that woman."

"Why go through the farce of an engagement, if Jessica wanted to split up with Jordan?" Becky mused. "They didn't have to announce it. They could have gone on dating."

I thought about Cam. I hadn't really looked at Jordan closely, or seen any photos of his. But there was no doubt, Cam was the more handsome of the brothers. I would bet my weekly stash of candy that Cam was the most handsome in the entire county.

"The other day, when I met Cam for dinner, he mentioned he would stay over at Jessica's."

Becky picked up on my meaning.

"And according to Colin Stevens, Jessica flirted around."

"Maybe she's just the friendly sort," I held up a finger.

"Yeah maybe," Becky said. "But Jordan could've felt threatened by it."

"So he didn't trust his own brother?" Tony mused. "Boy, am I glad I don't have one?"

"What about me?" Jeet called from the doorway.

He had the kind of hurt look only a teenager can have.

"I'll trust you with my life, bro. Any day!"

Tony did some kind of weird handshake with him and Jeet settled on a bar stool at the counter, happy to see the plate I'd set aside for him.

"Say Meera," Becky plunged ahead. "So Jordan thinks something's cooking between Cam and Jessica. He ups the ante by proposing to her."

"And Jessica accepts, even though she actually wants to break up with him?" I frowned.

"Saying yes would be a good way to prove she wasn't interested in Cam," Tony pointed out.

"But if she wasn't interested in Jordan either, why say yes at all?"

"Maybe she was buying some time. Or trying to avoid conflict between the brothers."

"Girls!" Tony flung his hands in the air. "Why are they so complicated? It seems to me, she was just playing around with everyone. What do you bet, her true intentions were something else entirely."

"You mean she sweet talked Cam, Jordan and Colin into thinking she was into each of them. But she actually was into someone else?"

"Some people have a hard time saying No. They just go along with whatever the other person says."

Jessica hadn't seemed like a wimp. She seemed strong enough to get her way. Maybe she was pulling a fast one over everyone, following her own agenda. That seemed more believable to me.

"I guess we have to talk to her first," I said. "And tell Stan about this. I wonder how he's coming along with the alibis."

"What about your program, Meera? Have you made any progress?" Becky asked.

I groaned, holding my stomach.

"I'm too stuffed to think of that right now."

"Who wants ice cream?" Jeet asked, scooping chocolate chip ice cream into a bowl.

We all wanted some.

Chapter 19

I pushed myself to work on the aging program later that evening. I collected a few photos of myself from 5 years ago. I took a current photo with the Logitech camera mounted on top of my desktop. This is what my program output should look like.

I wanted to run some tests myself before I gave a demo to anyone. I was afraid of failing miserably. Dad wouldn't like that. I had tested the modules, or small chunks of code as I created them. Every function worked well. But did it all come together as a whole?

I fed my old photo to the program and asked it to show me what I would look like now. I closed my eyes for a few minutes and dared myself to open them. I stared at the photo that looked back at me from the screen.

I suppose it could be my sister, except I didn't have one. The program had changed some of my features. It hadn't necessarily aged me. I did some analysis and changed a few parameters. The next result was better. I tweaked the program a bit more every time and a couple of hours passed.

Finally, I took a break for dinner.

"How's that aging progression module coming along, Meera?" Dad asked me.

"I'm close, but not perfect," I admitted.

"Don't be too hard on yourself, Meera. And don't try to be too precise. This is going to be a projection at best. Human beings don't age according to a formula. They have age spurts. And everyone ages differently."

I agreed with Dad. I was already finding it out.

"I'm running some preliminary tests, and you're right."

"Are you adding a constant factor for every year, or something variable depending on the age?" Dad launched into more detail.

"How do you mean?"

There are advantages for having a genius for a father, and there are the disadvantages.

"Well, aging a person from 10 to 20 is different from aging him from 40 to 50."

I thought for a moment and I agreed. I had missed this.

"So I need to check the starting age first, and then have different conditions …"

"Right!" Dad said. "And some people will age more around the eyes, or around the mouth. Some will go bald, or some will have a sagging chin. Some will have age spots. Depends on genetics, or health profile."

I was stunned.

"That's a whole lot of parameters, Dad! I'll never be done this way."

"Calm down, Meera. You don't have to be perfect. Do you not see what I'm trying to get at?"

Jeet spoke up, sounding bored.

"There is no single solution, sis! That's what Dad is trying to say."

I looked from Dad to Jeet, trying to make sense of their words. Dad had a silly grin on his face.

"The 19 year old has it, Meera."

I tried to hide my frustration. I ran away from the fancy future my family had planned for me. The one where I was going to be the next Bill Gates. But I didn't like it when someone made me look dumb. Especially my kid brother.

"Maybe I'm not cut out for this."

"You're too close to the problem, Meera. Change your perspective. Zoom out of the picture, eh?"

Dad winked.

It took me back to my childhood. One of the few times I had bonded with my father was when he set a puzzle for me to solve. He would give me clues, and then ask me to 'zoom out'.

Zooming out would make the image look smaller, but that wouldn't change its features. And like that, I had my Eureka moment.

"Ohhh! You mean there is no perfect solution. There are multiple solutions."

"Now you got it," Dad said happily.

What Jeet had easily grasped was that there was more than one correct answer to the problem. So I could apply a certain set of parameters and come up with one photo that showed pronounced aging around the mouth, another would show more lines on the forehead and so on. I could vary the amount of aging for each of these, based on the correction I applied. There could be hundreds of permutations and combinations.

"I have to go!" I sped back to my computer, eager to try out my latest idea.

A few minutes later, I was staring at a dozen pictures that looked a lot like me.

I tried the whole thing with my current photo and tried to see how I would look 10 years later. The results were not good for my vanity, but they pleased me. I wanted to test the program with as many different people as possible now. Pappa, Motee Ba and Dad would be great subjects.

I called Tony at midnight, waking him up.

"What is it, Meera?" he murmured.

"I need some photographs of you at different ages."

"Okay, later," he hung up.

I looked into Dad's office and found him sitting back in his chair, enjoying a glass of brandy.

"I need some photos for testing, Dad!"

He handed me a small box. He had already gathered photos of everyone in the house. The only ones missing were those of Mom. I wasn't ready for them yet.

I forced myself to sleep, letting my brain rest for a while. I was up before dawn, scanning in all the photos Dad had provided. I compared my program output of 40 year old Dad with an actual photo. Then I projected how he would look at 60. I did the same thing for Motee Ba at various stages.

Some of the output photos were very close to the mark. I applied some more correction to my program based on these results.

My program was almost perfect. I sat back, feeling a slight tremor in my hand. My heart thudded in my chest as I thought of what it meant. I was finally going to have a 'look' at my mother. Even if it was only in a photo.

My stomach rumbled and I decided to make some breakfast. I didn't have to go in to work so the day pretty much belonged to me. My aunt was flying in to spend some time with us. I had to go pick her up at the airport. With Christmas around the corner, that meant a shopping trip.

I chopped onions and tomatoes, and minced some jalapenos. Pappa walked in just as I placed a pan full of my spicy scrambled eggs on the table. He buttered his toast lavishly, taking advantage of Motee Ba's absence. She came in and flicked it out of his hand just as he was about to put it in his mouth. I tried to hide my smile.

"Are you coming to the city, Motee Ba?" I asked her.

She hesitated.

"I want to. But it's too cold out. I think I'll just stay in and make something special for dinner."

Becky bowed out so it was going to be just Tony and me. No way I was going alone to get Aunt Anita from the airport. She's a dragon, that one.

I had just finished clearing all the breakfast dishes when the phone rang.

"For you," Motee Ba beckoned.

It turned out to be Jessica.

"Hey Jessica. How are you? I didn't know you had this number."

"I got it from Pamela," she quipped. "Can we talk, Meera?"

"Let me call you back."

I guessed it was going to be a long call. I wanted to take it in the privacy of the guest house. I hurried over and called Jessica back.

"Good Morning Jessica," I greeted her. "I suppose you're back home in Texas?"

"What? No such luck. I'm where I always am. In my lab."

"Don't you have winter break?"

"Technically, I do, but there's a lot of work to be done. Research never stops, Meera. There's always some kind of urgency."

I nodded, then realized she couldn't see me. "Yeah!"

I knew that very well thanks to Dad and some of my own not so good experiences.

"So you're still in Swan Creek, you mean?"

"Unfortunately, yes. Usually I'm home by this time, busy shopping or baking cookies with my Mom, but with Jordan gone, none of it really makes sense."

I was quiet. I wondered how to disclose I was on to her.

She made it easy for me.

"Colin said he was chatting with you for quite a while yesterday."

"Sure was!"

She sucked in a deep breath and said urgently.

"Meera, we need to talk. Can you meet me today, please? Just name the place."

I really wanted to, but I couldn't dare be late for the flight.

"Sorry, I'm going out of town today. But I can give you 15 minutes now."

"Colin … he's a bit weird," she began.

I had gathered that on my own but I wanted her to go on.

"He's had a crush on me for a long time."

I maintained my silence, hoping Jessica would give me something solid.

"He's delusional," she burst out.

"Why are you telling me this?" I asked calmly.

"Did he talk about me, or Jordan?" she probed.

"Plenty!" I wasn't about to make it easy for her.

"Like what?" she said, almost hysterical.

"He told me you dated him for three years, and you were getting together with him. You didn't like Jordan at all. You flirt around with people and play with them. You were about to dump Jordan that day. You had a big fight with him …"

I paused to take a breath.

"It's not like the way you make it sound," she cried.

"Okay," I deadpanned.

"Look, I was with Colin for a few years. That part is true. That was when Jordan and I had broken up. But when I met Jordan again, we reconnected. We got back together. Colin didn't like that. He can be pretty controlling. He began to threaten me."

"What about breaking up with Jordan that day? Is that part true?"

"Sort of," Jessica admitted slowly.

"Why get engaged at all, and then break it off less than a week later?"

"I did love him, Meera. I was overjoyed when he proposed. I said yes in the heat of the moment. But I could never live on at the Triple H. And Jordan wasn't willing to move with me to Texas. That's what we were talking about that day, at Willow Lake."

"So you hung your engagement over him like bait?" I wasn't feeling the warm and fuzzies toward Jessica any more.

"Colin was giving me hell, threatening to reject all my work. I've been working hard at it for years."

"Was he blackmailing you? Is that what you're trying to say?"

Jessica let out a sigh.

"Look, it's hard to explain, but it was all overwhelming for me. I just want to get out of this town, you know. I can't do that until Colin approves my research. Once I get my PHD, I can do anything I want."

"Was Jordan in on this?"

"He wasn't. He couldn't be. He wasn't that great at hiding his emotions. Unless he stopped coming around, Colin was never going to believe I had dumped Jordan for real."

"So you were planning to dump Jordan, take up with Colin, get your degree, then dump Colin and then take up with Jordan again?"

My head was reeling.

"Yes, that's pretty much it," Jessica admitted.

I whistled.

"What about Cam?" I asked.

"What about him?" Jessica was surprised.

"You weren't, you aren't going around with him too?"

"Colin told you that, didn't he?" she asked sadly. "I think he must've said something to Jordan too."

"You think?" I asked, sarcastically.

"Do you see what I'm dealing with now? Colin Stevens is pure evil!"

Jessica sounded on the verge of tears.

"Evil enough to harm Jordan?" I dove in.

There was a stunned silence.

"You don't think ..." this time I could clearly hear Jessica's sobs.

"Doesn't matter what I think. You know the guy better. Was he in town that night?"

"In town?" Jessica wailed. "Meera, he was right there, in Willow Lake Park. He came to pick me up for my meeting."

I was speechless.

"Did he talk to Jordan that night?"

"He did. But I don't know what. I went to the restroom in the park. When I got back, they were glaring at each other. Colin's glasses were lying on the ground."

"I think you need to tell all this to the cops, Jessica," I advised, rubbing my hands across my forehead. "It's a lot to process, and I really need to get going now."

Jessica whimpered, but she recovered soon and thanked me. I promised to get in touch with her later that week. I needed to bring Stan up to speed on all this.

I collapsed on the couch, staring into space. How many more ants were hiding in the woodwork?

Chapter 20

My mind was churning, trying to process too much information. I definitely needed a break from Jordan Harris. Tony agreed to come with me. I looked forward to shopping my heart out in the mall before picking up my aunt from the airport.

Tony was driving his mom's sedan and I was settled into the passenger seat in my favorite pose. The seat back was reclined as far as it would go, my feet were up on the dash and I was munching Doritos like they were the last food left on earth.

I cursed as a semi nearly cut us off.

Tony laughed at me, and his eyes crinkled. I noticed how he got crow's feet around his eyes when he smiled. He was going to age around the eyes. Yes, I had begun noticing those fine signs of age people exhibited. When I do something, I live it.

"You're getting cranky from all that salt, Meera."

Tony grabbed the box of chips from my hand and chucked it behind his seat.

"Hey!" I protested.

"What's bothering you?" he asked.

"Too much information," I said cryptically. "I don't want to talk about it now," I said before Tony could ask me to elaborate.

The barren landscape was stark but beautiful. My bottom felt toasty in the heated seats and I snoozed on and off. Soon we were at the mall.

"We can shop together for a while, but then we need to split up."

I didn't want to miss this opportunity to get something good for Tony.

"What're you getting me this year?" Tony wiggled his eyebrows.

"You'll find out on Christmas morning, and not a day sooner."

I did my best to hide the presents but Jeet and Tony ferreted them out every year. It was like an ongoing contest.

I got cashmere sweaters for the men in the family. Dad and Jeet got V neck sweaters and Pappa got a cardigan. I got a silk scarf for Motee Ba and a pair of leather gloves. Her old ones were looking very worn. Becky got a bottle of her favorite perfume. I had a hard time choosing something for Tony.

"Hungry yet?" Tony asked.

We had split for half an hour and I tried to peek at the bag he held in his hand.

"Starving. Let's hit the food court here. We don't want to be late for the flight."

We got a mix of Chinese food, bourbon chicken, falafel, burgers and milk shakes. In short, a little bit of everything we could find there.

Aunt Anita was standing just inside the Arrivals area, one hand on her hip, her eyes hidden behind dark glasses. She had taken advantage of the full luggage allowance the airline permitted.

"About time," she said, opening her arms for a hug.

I went into them dutifully and kissed her on the cheek. Tony got a similar welcome.

My aunt is a formidable force in the family. She rules her own kids and husband, the Oklahoma Patels and Uncle Vipul and his California clan with an iron hand, all from her position of power in Edison, New Jersey. I never know what to expect from her.

She gave me a once over and nodded.

"A bit shabby but as pretty as ever."

I smiled. We got into the car and headed back to Swan Creek.

"Do you want to grab something from a drive through?" I asked solicitously.

"No need. I brought plenty of food."

She pulled out a box of *theplas*. Didn't I say they are a staple in any Gujarati household? Aunt Anita had slathered the *theplas* with *chundo*, a sweet and spicy mango relish and rolled them like cigars. She picked one up and started munching on it.

Tony and I grabbed one each.

Aunt Anita launched into a detailed report of what my cousins were up to.

"What's new with you, Meera?" she asked, finally coming up for air.

"Nothing much," I shrugged.

"Hmmm ... Ba doesn't say much on the phone. But I'll get to the bottom of things soon enough."

I had no doubt she would. Ba, her mother, is my Motee Ba or grandma. Tony took the exit for Swan Creek and we reached home a few minutes later. Motee Ba was sitting by the window. She rushed out, followed by Jeet.

"*Kem Cho, Ba?*"

Aunt Anita touched Motee Ba's feet and asked her how she was.

In Indian culture, we show our respect for parents and elders by touching their feet, or the ground they walk on.

Motee Ba and Aunt Anita laughed and cried, while happily wiping their tears. They do this every time they meet. Pappa had tottered out on his cane.

"Anita!" he bellowed.

Aunt Anita followed the same ritual again, touching Pappa's feet.

"Let's go inside. I'm freezing. Get the bags, boy!" he glared at Jeet who was engrossed in telling Tony something.

Everyone settled into the living room and I was dispatched into the kitchen to make the requisite tea, or chai.

"There's some *pakoras* I just finished frying," Motee Ba called out.

Aunt Anita squealed like a child.

They say nothing tastes as good as the food your Mom cooks. I have never eaten anything that fits this criteria, but yeah, I can vouch for anything my grandma cooks.

Dad was summoned and he came out, surprised at the sign of my aunt.

"Anita? What are you doing here?"

"Hello *Bhai*! I guess you forgot I was coming."

Aunt Anita smiled and hugged Dad.

The Christmas lights twinkled as the sun set. After a couple of rounds of tea, the ladies opted for wine and Dad poured Scotch for himself and Pappa.

I excused myself and went to the guest house. I was itching to talk to Stan. I called him up.

"Meera! Where have you been? I called earlier."

We exchanged some pleasantries and got to the point.

"I have loads of information," I told him. "So much that my head is reeling with this stuff."

"Calm down and tell me one by one," Stan soothed.

I told him about Colin Stevens. Stan hadn't heard of him until then, just as I suspected.

"How do you find these people, Meera? It's amazing."

"He was just there. And then he told me all these things."

"So Jessica and Jordan weren't really the love birds we thought they were," Stan burst out. "This puts a different spin on things. We never considered Jessica important until now."

"That's just the beginning."

I told him everything Colin Stevens had said. Then I told him what Jessica had said.

"So this piece of crap is blackmailing Jessica as we speak?" he thundered.

"Apparently, not any more. He doesn't need to, now that Jordan is out of the picture."

Stan was silent. I could imagine his frustration.

"Any luck with the alibis?" I asked him.

"Pamela Harris finally opened up," Stan laughed. "She was on a date."

"What? Then why didn't she say so?"

"It was all hush hush, it seems. She didn't want to say anything unless it was serious. But the man in question confirmed it."

"How do you know he isn't lying?" I asked.

I was curious about how the police decided who was speaking the truth and who wasn't.

"They were in a pub full of people until 11, twenty or so miles away from Swan Creek. And the guy dropped her off at the ranch around midnight. One of the ranch hands saw them."

"And Cameron?" I asked in a hushed voice.

"Unfortunately, he was spotted in Swan Creek that night. He was in a bar downtown around 9. After that, we don't know."

"What does he say about that?" I wondered how Cam would field this one.

"He admitted he stopped by for a drink. He had to. His leg was hurting so he drank a bit much. He slept it off at Jessica's and drove home around 6. He was doing his usual chores at the ranch when he heard about Jordan."

"My God, Stan! This just keeps getting better, doesn't it?"

"I know!" Stan sounded as tired as I did.

"Any more information on what caused Jordan's death?"

"Could be anything," Stan moaned. "We have come up with a questionnaire for the family. Some basic medical history and behavioral questions. The medical examiner's office hopes to get some kind of indication from it about what to test."

"Why do they need that?" I wanted to know.

"They tested for a few known poisons. Now there are 100s of substances they could test for. But we don't have the time or money to do that. Maybe this extra information will show them the way."

"What about the diner inspection?" I asked the question I dreaded most.

"Haven't you heard from Sylvie yet?" Stan was surprised. "The food guys swept the diner. They didn't find anything suspicious. The diner's cleared. I hear they are going to open for breakfast tomorrow."

"I was in the city all day. So maybe I missed this. That's the best news you could've given me, Stan."

I was really happy for Sylvie and Jon.

"Well, yes. I plan to be there bright and early tomorrow to see everything goes well. That, and it's been too long since I've had a taste of Sylvie's sausage gravy. I've actually lost a couple of pounds, you know."

The portly Stan Miller liked to eat.

"Don't worry. A few servings of my special fried chicken and you'll be back in the ring."

We were quiet for a moment.

"This case is turning out to be something, isn't it?" Stan muttered.

"It's all a big puzzle," I agreed. "I'm still not sure what the motive is. Money doesn't seem to be it."

I promised to keep Stan updated if I came across any more information.

Dinner time was noisy. Tony's mom had come over and we all enjoyed the special dinner that had been prepared for my Aunt.

"What's this I hear about you reopening Sarla's case, Meera?" my aunt asked me later.

Dad had gone back to his study. Pappa was dozing in his chair. He woke up suddenly when he heard my aunt's voice and snorted.

"About time!" he muttered, and nodded off again.

Motee Ba took my hand in hers, silently giving me courage.

I looked at my aunt.

"You've heard right, Aunt Anita."

"Are you prepared for what you might find?" she asked incredulously.

I didn't take her words to heart. I knew she was worried about how we would deal with the consequences.

"Well, we've lived without any news for 17 years. Maybe we'll finally get some closure."

I braced myself for a tirade. My Aunt Anita is not known to mince words.

"Are you encouraging her in this, Ba?" she accused her mother. "You should know better than that."

"Anita, we've all waited for a long time to get some kind of closure on this. I'm with Meera on this one."

My aunt glared at her father next. He ignored her. If anyone could stand up to my aunt, it was my grandpa.

"What about Andy? Does he know about this?"

"Dad's helping me a lot. He's handed over all his old files. I'm going through them now."

I was trying to be calm, but I was seething inside. My aunt always does this. She riles everyone up just a few hours after she lands.

"I'm warning you, Meera! No good can come of this."

"I know you're worried about all of us, Auntie. But you can't change my mind on this one."

She stood up, ready to storm out of the room.

"You're making a big mistake. Why don't you do something normal for a change? Like run after some boy your age?"

Motee Ba was looking tired.

"Sit down, Anita! You're too old for tantrums."

"Anything else you've been keeping from me, Ba?"

"Plenty," Motee Ba shot back. "For starters, Meera has a stalker."

Chapter 21

I banged around some pots and pans as I made breakfast. I was too mad at my aunt to make any special effort for her, but I had to be polite. I made spinach and feta omelets and made a cherry tomato sauce to go with them.

"Did you know Sylvie's is going to reopen today?" I asked Motee Ba.

She put her hand on her mouth.

"Oh my God, I forgot all about that."

She stood up and dialed the café's number from the kitchen phone. Sylvie answered and Motee Ba offered her congratulations.

"Too busy to talk right now," she told me. "There's a small number of people for breakfast, but they are prepping for a big lunch crowd."

"Maybe we should give them a helping hand," I mused.

Motee Ba was all smiles.

"See, when we went to Nancy's, we noticed all these special promos they were doing. Like free coffee refills if you spend over 10 bucks. Or soup and sandwich combos. Maybe we should do that in the beginning. Just until the old crowd gets used to going to the right diner!"

I raised my eyebrows at Motee Ba and she high fived me.

"Great idea, Meera!"

"School's out so no point posting any flyers there, but maybe we can just write these up on the chalk board?"

I was eager to get on to the diner and sound my new ideas off Sylvie.

"Go!" Motee Ba said, reading my mind.

I untied my apron and grabbed my keys. I could always have biscuits with gravy at Sylvie's.

"Where are you off to?" my aunt complained, walking into the kitchen.

I waved at her and kept going.

Sylvie's was a welcome sight. Jon was rubbing down the windows with some paper, and a big wreath hung on the door.

He grinned at me.

"Hello Meera. Thought we'd get into the holiday mood."

Becky was in the kitchen, humming to herself. She looked comfortable in her old domain. I hugged Sylvie and congratulated her.

"Guess they didn't find no rats in my kitchen," she smirked.

A few old timers were already working on their eggs and hash. They lifted their coffee cups and a cheer went up.

"I have an idea, Sylvie," I cut to the chase.

"Don't be shy, baby," she encouraged me.

"How about some special offers to get the place going again?"

I explained what I was thinking and we listed out different ideas.

"Are you still planning to supply pies to Nancy's?" I asked Sylvie.

She shook her head.

"Not anymore."

"We do need to push the pies again. How about a free coffee with every slice of pie? It can be a holiday special. I don't think anyone can resist that."

Sylvie got the idea.

"And let's offer a cup of soup with every sandwich."

"Are you planning to bankrupt me, woman?" Jon complained,

but the twinkle in his eye told me he was kidding.

"I think that's enough of a start," I nodded. "We'll have to make lots more soup."

"I'm on it," Becky called out from the kitchen.

"Has Stan been here yet? He was talking about missing your sausage gravy."

"He was here minutes after we opened," Sylvie laughed. "He dug into those buttermilk biscuits like there was no tomorrow."

"Things will turn around, Sylvie," I said softly, hugging her again.

We had all been through a rough time, but Sylvie and Jon had faced the brunt of it.

"Any more ideas on what happened to that boy?" she asked.

I shook my head. I helped Becky for a few hours and headed home. I looked in on Tony on the way back.

"What's cookin', good lookin'?" he teased.

"Any guesses what Pam's alibi is?"

"Just say it," Tony said.

He doesn't like these guessing games.

"She has a beau!"

"You should've thought of that!" Tony kidded, but he was half serious.

"Want to come and check out my aging program?" I asked Tony.

"Are you ready to demo it already?" his eyes gleamed.

"As ready as I'll ever be."

We drove home and I fired up the computer in the guest house. I fed in a photo of Aunt Reema's from when Tony was born. I ran the program and it spit out 10 different photos of Aunt Reema as she should look now.

Tony was speechless.

"Why do they all look different?"

I explained how each photo was a projection of a peculiar combination of aging parameters. Two or three of the photos looked very much like Aunt Reema as she looked now. The others were a good likeness.

"It's like a portrait," Tony exclaimed. "Some artists get it exactly right, while some are almost right."

I laughed.

"Yeah, sort of. The trouble is we don't know which one is going to be right, or most right, in my Mom's case. That's why I've come up with this option of getting 10 possible results."

"You mean you want to pass around 10 photos instead of just 1," Tony summed up.

"Exactly!"

"As long as the people you give these to don't mind, that should work well."

"You think I'm ready to show this to Dad?"

Tony's response was a bone crushing hug. I took that as a Yes.

The guest house soon filled up with the entire family. Aunt Anita sat in a corner chair with a frown on her face. Apparently, she still hadn't forgiven me.

"Get on with it, girl," Pappa tapped his cane.

I started with a photo of Motee Ba and fed it to the program. Everyone gasped at the 10 photos the program spit out. I followed with a photo of Dad, Jeet and Pappa. Finally, I fed a photo of my Mom.

The silence in the room was deafening. The photo was in profile so I didn't expect much from it.

"I've never tried running the program with a side shot," I

mumbled.

Before I finished speaking, the screen was splashed with 10 different photos. I looked at the screen in dismay. For some reason, the software hadn't worked well in this case. Many features were distorted and I ended up with what looked like funny caricatures.

Dad looked disappointed.

"You've done an excellent job, Meera," he said kindly. "But we need a better photo. Or you need to fix the code."

My aunt spoke up.

"This is like magic. You're a genius, Meera."

No one commented on that. Being a genius isn't enough in my family.

"I think I have a front facing photo of your mother," Aunt Anita announced. "Now I just have to remember where it is, and then have someone back home scan it and send it to me."

I looked at her hungrily.

She spoke to Dad.

"You remember the photos we took at the airport when you were going to the US for the first time? Sarla's staring straight at the camera in that one."

Dad had paled a bit. He licked his lips and blinked at his sister.

Aunt Anita nodded at me.

"Don't worry, Meera. I'll get it for you."

Motee Ba was gently wiping her eyes. Even Jeet looked disturbed. Everyone had realized that we would soon be privy to what my mother might have looked like now. It was an eerie feeling. We didn't know if such a person existed or if it was a ghost.

"Hansa! It's time for my lunch!" Pappa roared, breaking the

tension.

Everyone dispersed. Tony and I stayed on, along with Jeet.

"You're close, Meera," he said in a hushed voice.

"This is just a photo, Jeet!"

I was close alright. Close to tears. The phone rang and I picked it up.

"For you, Meera," Motee Ba said and hung up the extension.

"Meera, Hello, can you hear me?" Pamela Harris came on the line.

"How are you Pam?" I asked.

"The cops asked for my alibi. And I had to tell them. So I guess there's no harm in telling you now."

I felt uncomfortable.

"I sort of know, Pam!"

"Oh? I suppose you spoke to that cop friend of yours?"

Pam took my silence for a yes.

"Now you know why I didn't want to talk about it," she sighed.

"I understand. Everyone's entitled to their privacy."

"It's not just that. I'm ashamed!"

"Why?" I was curious.

"Can you imagine having a beau at my age? I'm too old. What will Pa say?"

Pam may not be too old to date, but she was certainly too old to worry about what her Pa thought. I didn't say a word.

"I used to go out with someone, back when Ma was alive. Then I got busy taking care of the boys. I never met anyone. Until now, that is."

"Relax, Pam," I crooned. "No one's judging you."

"Jordan would've been happy for me," she sniffled. "He always tried to make me go out and meet people."

"Hey, have they given you some kind of questionnaire about him?"

Pam sniffled again, taking a deep breath.

"I just spoke to that policeman. They are going to be faxing it over soon. Do you want to come over and help me go through it?"

"I'm not sure I can help. You're the one that knew him."

"Please. I'll be glad of the company."

"Let me get back to you," I promised.

I asked Tony if he was up for a ride to the Triple H. We had nothing much going on anyway. I called Pam back and told her we'd start after lunch.

Jeet wanted to tag along and I agreed reluctantly.

"Maybe I can ride a horse today. We missed doing that when they kicked us out."

"You'll do no such thing. We are going there for work, Jeet. And Pam's already refunded our money from that time."

"What?" Jeet pounced. "Where is it?"

"It's gone!" I laughed, making a face at him.

"Bet she bought some fancy gift for you with it," he accused Tony.

We piled into Tony's pickup after lunch. I wondered why Pam couldn't fill out that questionnaire on her own. I decided to take this chance to ask her about Cam and Jessica.

Jeet kept Tony busy in some guy talk all the way. I was bored to death by the time we drove through the arches of the Triple H.

Pam had asked us to come to the homestead.

Pa Harris was ensconced in his rocking chair, and a fire was blazing. I was glad because the temperature was beginning to drop quite a bit. Pam poured coffee, looking excited.

The lack of any holiday decorations was obvious at the Triple H.

Pa Harris must have been thinking the same thing. He nodded toward an empty corner.

"That's where we usually put our tree. Jordan had a good lot going over at the west border of the ranch. We get at least an eight foot fir every year. One year, it was so tall, the tops brushed the rafters."

He seemed lost in some old memory, his eyes looking sunken and empty. I didn't have an appropriate response so I stayed quiet.

Pam picked up a sheaf of papers held together by a clip.

"This is what they faxed over. I hope we can answer most questions without having to go to our old family doc."

I leaned forward, reading the questions as Pam checked them off one by one.

"Heart disease, No. Hypertension – No. Jordan was very calm most of the time but his temper could flare up in an instant."

I tried to peek at the next question.

"Cholesterol? Borderline."

Pam went over questions related to almost every bodily function.

"How is any of this going to help?" she began looking frustrated.

I noticed something about the papers she was holding.

"Look, Pam, these papers are all mixed up. You need to start from Page 1 and go through them in the right order. Maybe that will make some more sense?"

"You're right, Meera!" She slammed the papers in my hand. "Can you do it, please? Then we'll take it from the top again."

Pam looked like she was about to burst into tears, or blow a gasket, so I obliged.

"Okay! Was Jordan allergic to penicillin?" I asked.

She shook her head no.

I moved to the next question.

"Was he allergic to any drugs?"

"No. But he was allergic to nuts."

Pam's response was as casual as telling me she took two sugars in her tea.

"That's the next question," I said, looking up, suddenly afraid of what was coming.

Was subject allergic to any food items, such as milk or nuts?

Pam's eyes widened and she covered her mouth with one hand.

"I never thought of that."

"What kind of Southerner doesn't eat pecan pie?" Pa Harris said mournfully. "But my Jordan could never abide by it, ever since he was a child."

"What kind of pie did they find on him?" Pam asked urgently.

"Er, I'm not sure, but I think it was a berry pie."

The image of Jordan sprawled on that bench was crystal clear in my mind. So were the pie crumbs with the reddish filling, and the wedge of pie that was falling out of his pocket.

"Do you think it's important?" Pam asked.

"Let's send in the questionnaire. We'll let the police do their job."

I was trying to be nonchalant but I was sure we'd hit upon the cause of Jordan's death.

Chapter 22

Pamela couldn't usher us out fast enough. I still wanted to ask her about Cam.

"Was Cam interested in Jessica?" I asked her point blank.

She looked shocked. I didn't think she had thought about this before.

"How do you mean? Do you mean was he romantically involved with her?"

"Unhunh," I nodded my head vigorously.

"What made you say that?"

"Look, Pam, maybe it's nothing. I may be mistaken."

She stuck to her stance.

"What made you say that, Meera?"

"Well, he mentioned staying over at her place once or twice. In fact, that's where he was the day Jordan ... I mean, the day Jordan and Jessica celebrated their engagement."

Pam's face settled into a mask.

"I wouldn't know anything about that."

"Please, Pam, if you know something, you should tell me now."

Pam hesitated.

"Jessica was, is, the friendly type. She was free with her favors."

My eyebrows shot up my head.

"Do you mean to say she slept around?"

"What?" Pam's face looked stricken. "Not those kind of favors! Anything, really. She never said no to anyone. Kids at the college had keys to her apartment, to her car. They raided her fridge anytime they felt like it. And I think they also raided her wallet."

"You mean she couldn't say No to people."

Pam shrugged.

"Another way of putting it. Look, she was Daddy's girl. And Daddy's rich. Those kids knew that and they took advantage."

"What about Cam?"

"I suppose Cam did it to hassle Jordan," Pamela finally admitted.

"Isn't that taking their rivalry too far?"

"That's the way they were. Cam insisted Jessica would have chosen him if she'd seen him first."

"She could still have chosen him, don't you think?" I mused.

"But she got engaged to Jordan!" Pamela shook her head. "Why would she do that if she fell for Cam?"

"Maybe she was just buying time? Maybe she thought Cam would step up if he thought time was running out."

"I don't know, Meera," Pam was uncertain.

"Jessica wanted to move to Texas. What do you think of that?"

Pamela's face blanched.

"What? Was Jordan moving with her too? Pa would be crushed."

"I hear Jordan wasn't ready to," I eased her mind. "Do you think Cam's unwanted attentions may have made her want to flee?"

Jessica had told me they fought over leaving the Triple H, but she hadn't explained why. Maybe the thought of having Cam around her all the time made her uncomfortable.

Pamela clutched her head with her hands. I felt sorry for her. I was experiencing something similar, trying to make sense out of this.

"Meera, I think I'm going to send in the questionnaire to your police friend. And let them investigate. I just can't think any more."

I nodded. We said goodbye and Tony started driving back.

"You think I gave her a hard time?" I asked Tony.

"Let's just drive back home, okay?" he said. "No stopping for snacks anywhere."

We reached home in an hour, and of course we were starving by that time.

"I hope Granny's got something to eat," Tony said, rubbing his hands.

Jeet let out a yawn. He had napped all the way back. A car pulled into our driveway and stopped a few yards from us.

"Looks like Motee Ba's just coming in too," I observed.

We piled out, watching Motee Ba and Aunt Anita get out of their car. Their eyes were shining and they seemed about to burst. Like they wanted to use the bathroom really bad.

"Let's go inside, Meera!"

My aunt held my arm in an iron grip and almost dragged me behind her.

"Sit," she ordered, pointing to the couch.

"What's the matter?"

"Ba told me about this person that's stalking you," Aunt Anita began with relish. "I came up with an idea."

We all groaned. My aunt was never short on ideas. Most of the time, they involved gossip or snooping.

"We decided to follow you," Motee Ba gushed.

"You followed us all the way to the Triple H?" Tony exclaimed. "That's a two hour drive Granny!"

Motee Ba cracked her knuckles. She only did that when she was agitated.

"We followed you all the way there. Then we drove on and

doubled back. We stopped by the side of the road until we saw you start back. Then we followed you home."

"And?" I asked, bored.

I didn't expect much from this fool endeavor.

"You had a tail, Meera. No doubt about it."

My aunt sounded triumphant.

"Maybe that person was just driving on the same road, going somewhere else?"

Aunt Anita held up a finger.

"In that case, why would they wait for you and follow you back?"

"Wait a minute, Auntie. So there were two cars just idling at the side of the road. You must have noticed each other. And I should have noticed you."

Tony was probably mad because he hadn't spotted them. We had been too busy talking.

"Well, I drove off the shoulder a bit and ..." Motee Ba stopped mid sentence.

"Did you wait in a ditch?" I asked. "Unbelievable!"

"It wasn't a ditch," she protested. "Well, not exactly. It was just a bit off the road. There were a few bushes that gave us perfect cover."

I rolled my eyes.

"And what about the other car then?" Tony demanded.

"She went into a small country store," Aunt Anita began.

"We know the place." I told her about our last visit to that store, and what the woman there had said.

"We had the perfect spot!" Motee Ba said proudly. "We spotted you come out of that turnoff that takes you to the Triple H.

Then when you passed the country store, we saw this car pulling out behind you. We followed."

"What about the car?"

"That car was behind you until you turned into our lane. Then it drove past."

I felt numb.

"Was it a woman, then? Are you sure?"

Aunt Anita nodded.

"Pretty sure. And I don't see a man from these parts wearing pink."

"Can you recognize her?" Tony asked eagerly.

Both Motee Ba and Aunt Anita hung their heads.

"She had some kind of scarf wrapped around her head and face. As if she's driving in a car without heat. I couldn't even spot her hair color."

My aunt sounded beaten. Motee Ba didn't look too great either. I tried to cheer them up.

"But you spotted her!! Don't you see? All this time, we've only had suspicions. Even the cops haven't actually seen her follow me."

"You need to call Stan right now, Meera," Motee Ba said urgently.

I didn't waste any time. Stan was brought up to speed.

"Your granny did this?" Stan was incredulous. "You Patels are turning into quite the sleuths."

"What now?" I pressed.

"Nothing much," Stan said. "I don't suppose your granny got the plates on that car?"

I asked Aunt Anita and she handed me a piece of paper. I rattled it off to Stan.

"I'll get on it. My guess is this is a rental, just like the last time. But maybe we'll get some more info on it this time."

"Have you heard from Pam?"

I told him about Jordan's nut allergy and told him to expect something from Pam soon.

"Maybe this is the clue we've been missing, Meera," Stan perked up. "We can test for this now."

"We still need to find out who did it, Stan," I reminded him. "Isn't that more important?"

"That's the ultimate goal alright. But knowing the method of the crime might help us narrow it down."

I thanked Stan and hung up.

"I'm starving!" Aunt Anita said.

"Hey, that's my line," Jeet said, and we all burst out laughing.

"Let's order pizza," I suggested.

Pizza sounded great to everyone, and we put in an order for two large pies.

"Any luck finding that photo, Auntie?" I almost wanted her to say no.

"Haven't checked my email since breakfast," my aunt replied. "Let me have a bite to eat first, Meera!"

I almost sighed with relief. Dad joined us reluctantly when the pizza arrived.

"Your mother's losing her mind," Pappa roared at him. "You need to control these women better, boy."

Motee Ba tried to skim over their covert mission. Dad's mouth dropped open.

"This is exactly what you do every time you come here," Dad

looked at my aunt accusingly.

Then he stared at his mother.

"But Ba! You're supposed to keep an eye on them, not join their ranks."

Motee Ba ignored him, choosing to keep her mouth shut. My Dad offered some more choice words for everyone and then dug into his pizza.

"Can I check my email on your computer, Andy?" Aunt Anita asked Dad.

He stood up and she followed him into his office. She was back a few minutes later, her face covered in smiles. She came and put a hand on my shoulder.

"Just emailed it to you, Meera."

The tension in the room went up a notch.

"Are you ready?" Motee Ba asked quietly.

I was as ready as I would ever be.

Tony and Jeet followed me to the guest house. I told the others to wait for my call.

My hands shook as I opened my aunt's email. The photo was the sort I needed, although it wasn't very sharp. I downloaded it to my hard drive and fired up my program.

I looked at Tony and Jeet and took a deep breath. None of us dared to say a word. Tony folded an arm around me, and Jeet did the same. I hit the Enter key on my keyboard and closed my eyes until Tony gently prodded me.

"It's done, Meera!"

Ten images stared back at me from the screen. If my mother were alive, she would look something like this.

I picked up the extension and called Motee Ba over. They came over, Pappa tapping his cane impatiently, leaning on Dad. I pointed to the screen unnecessarily. There was a shocked silence and tears rolled down the women's eyes.

Dad cleared his throat.

"I think you can send these on now, Meera."

"Would you pick any particular ones out of these?"

All of them pointed to the same two pictures.

"Alright then, I'll get on with this."

I wanted everyone to leave so I could launch into a full blown crying session. They all seemed to have the same idea. The group split up and only Tony stayed behind. He opened his arms wide as soon as we were alone.

"You can let go now," he said softly.

The tears began to flow, and I began sobbing my heart out. I couldn't fathom what had just happened or why it was painful. Maybe seeing how my mother would have looked now had made me feel her loss all over again.

"All this time, and it still hurts to think of her," I muttered through my sobs.

Tony heated some water for tea and dunked in a chamomile tea bag. He made me drink the tea.

"You need to be strong, Meera," he soothed. "There's nothing wrong with being emotional. But now you have to take the next step."

I put all the 10 photos into a zip folder and prepared a cover letter for them. I emailed this out to the list of people who had already replied to me. I would also include it in the new queries I sent out after this.

"What a day!" Tony exclaimed. "We may have found what killed Jordan, we know you have a stalker for sure, and now this."

"A bit too much for you?" I asked.

Sometimes I worry Tony will get tired of me and stop hanging out.

"Not yet," he teased.

Chapter 23

I spent most of the next day contacting authorities in different states. I sent out the photos to dozens of people. Most of them would be busy with the holidays, ready to take their annual time off. So there was a fat chance any of them would read my email before the New Year. But I wanted to get the photos out before I had any second thoughts.

There was a hum of activity around the house. Motee Ba and my aunt were rustling up treats in the kitchen, talking about old times, catching up on gossip from the extended family. Even as a child, I had loved sitting at the kitchen table with them, shelling peas or helping them somehow, soaking up their stories of life in India. And then there was my aunt's life in New Jersey. Sometimes, it seemed to me like she lived in a mini India in the heart of Jersey.

My Dad had finished sending out grades and seemed to have a gap in his calendar. He offered to help me with the Mom Project.

I wanted to gather Tony and Becky and go over everything we had learned so far about Jordan Harris. I was going around in circles. Nothing made much sense. Every person close to him seemed to be telling the truth. Either one of them was a seasoned liar, or there was someone who hadn't come out of the wings yet. So far, I hadn't been able to discern any motive. Far as I could tell from my vast collection of Agatha Christie books, there is always a motive for murder.

I called Jessica on a whim and asked if she could meet me. She suggested the coffee shop on campus. Fifteen minutes later, I had parked in the deserted lot outside the Student Union. Jessica was already waiting for me with two coffees and cookies.

"I got you a latte," she pointed. "Is that okay?"

"Sure!" I thanked her and picked up a cookie.

Cookies speak a language I understand. They always cry 'pick me up'.

"So what's up, Meera?" Jessica got to the point.

She looked tired. She had dropped a few pounds since the first time I met her and the circles under her eyes had darkened. Her hair was dry like it gets when you run out of conditioner. I didn't know if she was always so unkempt.

"I went to the ranch yesterday," I began.

"Pam called me last night," Jessica nodded. "And she told me about that questionnaire."

She leaned closer to me.

"Do you remember the first time we met? I had told you how Jordan always got the berry pie at Sylvie's because he couldn't eat pecans."

I shook my head.

"All this time, even Sylvie didn't mention anything about a possible allergy."

"Jordan's been eating at Sylvie's for years. I guess they knew him by face. There's no way anyone there would hand him a pie that had nuts in it."

"What are you saying, Jessica?"

"If they find nuts in Jordan's body …" she paused and held back a sob. "If they find nuts, I think we can be sure it was done on purpose. There's no way Jordan would eat nuts by accident. He was very careful about it."

I placed a hand on her shoulder.

"Let's wait until we know for sure."

"Is this what you wanted to talk about?" she asked.

"You told me you wanted to move away from the Triple H," I began. "But I don't think you mentioned why."

"I'm an only child. And my Daddy has a big spread down South. We could do our own thing there."

"But I thought the resort at Triple H was Jordan's baby. Didn't he bring the ranch up to snuff by himself?"

"Jordan put a lot of sweat into the Triple H. But he wasn't really the boss. He had to get his Pa's permission before taking any decision. And then talk to Pam and get her approval. It could get tedious."

"What about his brother?" I asked.

"He didn't chime in on day to day stuff when he was away," Jessica said, "but he was beginning to take an interest, now that he's planning to settle here."

"So that was an additional person to please," I noted.

"Yep!" Jessica pursed her lips.

"And you're saying Jordan didn't like doing that," I repeated.

Jessica frowned.

"Jordan was a ninny. A pushover. He hardly ever noticed how his family was taking advantage. He put his brains and brawn into the Triple H, and he didn't have much to show for it."

I gave her a sympathetic smile. It seemed like Jessica was the one who didn't want to have Jordan's family around her. I didn't think she'd gone to the trouble of getting a doctorate just to check in guests at a dude ranch.

"Isn't your research something to do with cows?" I asked.

She smiled brightly. "We're close to developing a supplement that will naturally hasten their growth. I'm working on a pilot with a small herd on Daddy's ranch. We've had very good results. This will almost double our output."

"Why didn't Jordan want to move?" I asked.

Jessica twisted her mouth in a grimace.

"He didn't want to leave his family. As if we were moving across the world. My Daddy's ranch is barely a 100 miles away from the H."

"Pa Harris talked about how old their ranch is," I murmured.

Jessica got excited.

"That's just it. Jordan kept on about that all the time. And he wanted to reconnect with his brother."

"Speaking of Cameron …" I paused, knowing my next line might annoy Jessica. "Do you like him?"

"You mean like, do I want to go out with him?" Jessica asked.

I gave a slight nod.

"I'm not that kind of girl, Meera. You think I would get engaged with one brother and go out with the other?"

"Did he come on to you?" I persisted.

"Guys come on to me all the time. What can I do? With Cam, I think it was more for shock effect."

"He mentioned he has a key to your apartment."

"No he doesn't. But I do keep it under a potted plant right outside my door. Things aren't that formal on campus. I live close to the lab. So people often just crash at my place for a nap. Cam did it too a couple of times. No big deal."

"He said he was at your place the night Jordan … that night."

I raised my eyebrows at Jessica.

"Maybe he was. I was working through the night. Then I napped at my desk and got home around 7."

I didn't think I would get much more out of Jessica.

"Are you going home for Christmas?" I asked.

"I'm leaving on Christmas Eve. Trying to squeeze in as much work as possible until then."

I stood up and wished her a safe drive home. She hugged me impulsively. Then she turned and walked away.

I nursed my coffee for a while more, enjoying the solitude in a place that was usually bustling with plenty of people. I dumped my empty coffee cup into a trash can and walked out, planning to visit Sylvie's on my way home.

I almost ran into Colin Stevens. He seemed to be wearing the same clothes, and looked more unwashed than before.

"Finished your meeting?" he asked.

"What?" I burst out.

"Your meeting with Jessica? How was it?"

Colin Stevens had managed to irritate me once again. I opened my mouth to give him a piece of my mind.

"Didn't I say she tells me everything?" he sneered.

"That, or you eavesdrop on her phone calls," I said mildly.

"Who do you think she called when she wanted a ride, hunh?" he asked, pushing his glasses up his nose. "Who did she turn to when that so called fiancé of hers was sulking over something stupid?"

"Are you talking about the night Jordan died?" I asked.

He puffed up, looking important.

"Do you realize you may have been the last person to see him alive?"

"Of course not!" he retorted. "I mean, of course I wasn't."

"You would say that of course. To save your skin."

Colin Stevens laughed in my face.

"You work at the library, don't you? Been reading a lot of trashy novels? Why would I want to save my skin?"

I shook my head.

"Forget it. What do you mean you weren't the last person to talk to him?"

"We had an urgent team meeting that night. Our funding depends on delivering results at a certain pace. Every person needs to pull their weight and be present at the meetings. Jessica had promised to be there by 7. We needed to prep before our 8 PM meeting with our industry sponsor. When she wasn't in by 7:30, I called her."

"Go on," I urged.

Colin Stevens had stopped to take a breath.

"I could hear Jordan cursing in the background. Apparently, they were in the middle of an argument. Jessica asked me to come pick her up. When I reached there, they weren't talking to each other. Jessica went to use the restroom."

"Did Jordan say anything?" I asked.

"He looked pretty angry. He wasn't good to me at the best of times, so I didn't say anything. He opened his truck and took out a box or something."

My blood pressure went up a notch.

"Was it like the box they wrap pies in?" I asked with bated breath.

"How would I know?" Colin pounced. "I was reading some of our test results. We really were on a tight deadline."

"Then?"

"I heard Jordan call out to someone. Sounded like he was surprised to see that person there. I think it was his brother."

"Did you see this person?" I asked.

Colin Stevens shook his head. "I told you I was busy studying something. I thought maybe Jordan was just crying out, or was drunk. Then I saw a guy somewhere in the shadows. He beckoned to Jordan and he walked away."

"What about Jessica?"

"Jessica got into my car and we raced back to campus with 5 minutes to spare."

"Was Jessica in the lab all night then?"

"We all were," Colin smiled. "We pulled an allnighter, and then went home in the morning."

Colin had managed to add something to the story again. I wondered who it was Jordan had talked to. Was it really his brother Cameron? Or was it just some random guy in the park. Maybe it was some homeless person who wanted a bite to eat.

"Have you talked to the police yet?" I asked Colin Stevens. "I'm sure they will appreciate all the valuable information you have."

Colin Stevens whipped out a card.

"They can talk to me anytime. So can you. Let me know if you have any more questions."

I took his card and put it inside my purse.

"Say Jessica and Jordan had a falling out," I mused. "What do you think she would do?"

"The real question you want to ask is would Jessica do anything to harm Jordan, right?" Colin Stevens gave me a dark look.

I pursed my lips. I didn't want to say yes.

"I'll answer anyway. She would've dumped him some time or the other. He wasn't smart enough for her. Or ambitious enough."

Soon, Colin would be extolling his own virtues as the perfect match for Jessica. I thanked him for his patience and stepped out of the building.

The cold air felt invigorating and I took a deep breath. Once again I was overwhelmed with the sheer amount of information floating around. Was there anyone who knew all the facts? Or anyone who could make sense out of this mess?

I got into the Camry and hit the road. I was so lost in my thoughts, I found myself in our driveway about 15 minutes later. I had completely forgotten my plan to visit Sylvie's.

The spicy notes of ginger and garlic wafted out from our kitchen, along with the scent of assorted spices. Dinner was almost ready and I was just in time for it.

Chapter 24

The next couple of days were busy sampling all the yummy food Motee Ba cooked for my aunt. It was the holidays, after all. Jeet and Pappa added in some special requests. Even my Dad wasn't immune to the delicacies that came out of the kitchen at regular intervals.

"What're we doing for Christmas dinner?" my aunt asked the room in general.

We were gathered around in the living room, playing cards. There was a roaring fire in the grate. We were well insulated against the sub zero winds blowing outside.

We were drinking mulled cider, and it warmed me inside out. I groaned mentally as I realized my aunt would be with us for Christmas day too. I love my aunt, but she can be a trial. She had already sneaked in about a dozen photos of eligible young men by me. They were all Indian and extremely well educated from Top 10 schools. Some were born and raised in America while some were still in India. Almost all of them were surgeons or doctors of some kind. The least desirable of them was a lawyer.

"You're not getting any younger, Meera. Once you cross 25, no one will look at you."

I showed the appropriate fear this statement was supposed to evoke.

"You're mocking me, aren't you?" my aunt asked suspiciously.

"No, I'm not, Aunt Anita!" I protested without much conviction.

"I like Tony too, but he hasn't pulled his life together yet," she responded.

"What does that mean?" I sighed. "Where's Tony come into all this?"

Motee Ba and my aunt exchanged a look. They didn't bother to reply.

"Anand's department buddies usually invite us for Christmas dinner," Motee Ba told my aunt. "But I don't think we have an invite yet this year."

"They had to go out of town to visit a sick relative," Dad explained. "I was supposed to tell you this."

"We've got to do something!" Motee Ba straightened in her chair, looking hopeful.

"Please, Ba! No more parties …"

Even a small party ends up being fifty people and is at least 3-4 days of work.

"Why don't we do a potluck?" I asked. "With Jon & Sylvie and Tony's people if they are free?"

"Not a bad idea!" Motee Ba leapt up and dialed Sylvie.

"We're meeting tomorrow to talk about it."

She held up a hand, warding off my Dad as he opened his mouth to speak.

"Everyone's going."

No one argued because we had all looked forward to doing something special for the holidays.

The next day, we were seated at Sylvie's, drinking coffee and eating pie.

"It's nice to see everyone here after so long," Sylvie smiled.

"Mom can make the roast," Tony volunteered, then looked at his Mom.

She nodded.

We came up with a short menu and then started splitting up the dishes amongst us.

My gaze strayed around the diner. A few tables were occupied.

People were busy eating their food, talking softly amongst themselves or reading the paper. Becky was busy in the kitchen, filling orders.

A couple of cars pulled up outside. I braced myself as I realized they were police cars. Stan Miller got out of one car, and walked toward the diner door. Three other deputies flanked him. He pushed open the heavy door and strode in.

He seemed taken aback at seeing all of us.

"Hello Meera," he stuttered, looking tense.

"What's the matter?" I asked fearfully.

"It's not good," he said to me, almost under his breath.

Stan Miller turned toward Jon. Two of his henchmen had already surrounded Jon. One stood near the diner door.

"I'm sorry Jon, but you'll have to come with me."

Sylvie moved closer to Jon and took his hand in hers.

"What's going on?" she asked Stan, bewildered.

"Some more tests were done on Jordan Harris. They found nuts in his stomach, along with berries. Looks like the last thing he ate was your pie."

"But haven't you already cleared us?" Sylvie asked in a rush.

She had begun to hyperventilate.

"The food department checked the diner for chemicals or poisons. Or rat infestation. They didn't check for nuts, but I'm sure you have those around."

"We sure do, yes sir!" Sylvie was defensive. "My pecan pie is our top seller. But I didn't give that boy any. I know he never eats them nuts."

"So maybe there was some cross contamination?" Stan said reluctantly. "Look, Sylvie, I've been eating that pie for years. I know there's nothing wrong with it. But I have to take Jon with me now. I'm sorry."

"But it's two days to Christmas!" Sylvie wailed, hugging Jon tightly.

"I know. I'm sorry."

Stan looked uncomfortable.

I was impressed by Stan's behavior. The old Stan would have come in with sirens blaring, and ordered his people to take Jon away. He was really maturing a bit. That didn't make the situation any easier, though.

Dad stood up and patted Jon on the shoulder.

"I don't think you have a choice."

"So, are you arresting me?" Jon had been silent so far.

Stan Miller sighed deeply. Then he gave a slight nod.

"Jon Davis. You are under arrest for the murder of Jordan Harris. You have the right to remain silent. Anything you say …"

A gasp went around as Stan Miller read Jon his rights. We were all speechless as the deputies marched Jon out and put him in the back seat of a police cruiser. They backed out slowly and sped away.

Sylvie burst into sobs, and Motee Ba rushed to console her.

"Don't you have that lawyer's number in your phone?" Motee Ba asked Dad.

She was referring to the time earlier in the year when Stan had wanted to arrest me. My Dad had contacted a city lawyer at that time and I hoped he hadn't deleted his number from his phone.

Dad was already flicking through the address book in his phone.

He stepped away and spoke to someone for about five minutes.

"The lawyer can be here right away, but it won't help much. The courts are closed for the holidays. The earliest anything can be done is on Tuesday the 26th."

Sylvie gasped and clutched her heart. She was crying openly now.

"So my Jon's going to be in Jail over Christmas?"

Motee Ba put an arm around her and tried to placate her. Aunt Reema did the same. My Aunt Anita had a frown on her face. She can be a bit stuck up at the best of times. She doesn't get how close we are to Sylvie and Jon.

The few guests in the diner were staring at the scene openly, their food forgotten. Becky had come out of the kitchen. She tried to steer the guests to their food or urged them to leave if they were done.

Tony, Jeet and I were quiet. There wasn't much to say anyway.

Motee Ba looked up and beckoned me closer. Her mouth was set in a firm line and there was a determined glint in her eye.

"Do something, Meera. Find out who did this."

I felt the weight of responsibility settle on my shoulders. So far, I had been serious about finding out what happened to Jordan. But now the stakes had gone up. The clock was ticking and someone close to me was affected.

"I'm going to do my best," I promised, clasping Sylvie's hand in mine.

Dad and Pappa looked at each other. But they didn't say anything this time.

I was very familiar with the kitchen at Sylvie's. I generally manned the grill with Becky. There was a small room that Sylvie used exclusively for baking. She took me in there and showed me the setup again.

"Look, I have separate ovens for baking my pecan pies or any other nut based pies. There's another oven for the fruit pies. This here shelf on the right holds the fruit pies and the one on the left holds the pecan pies. All the utensils are different too."

I was impressed. I hadn't known Sylvie was this meticulous about the issue.

"Cross contamination is almost impossible here," I agreed.

"But if there's no contamination, what's the alternative?" Motee Ba wondered. "Will they say it was done on purpose?"

"We need to find out who had access to the pie," I marked, "both here in the diner and outside the diner."

"Well, he certainly had his fill here," Becky noted. "He ate a whole piece of pie with ice cream, and then he took half a pie with him."

"What time did he have dinner here?" I wanted to refresh my memory.

"Around 6-6:30," Becky confirmed.

"We know he was well until almost 8-8:30. So maybe someone doctored the pie that he took along with him."

"But who? And why?" Motee Ba pounced. "The why's not important to us. We just need to know who did it so we can exonerate Jon."

"The why is going to help us in finding out who did it," I told her.

"What's our next move, Meera?" Tony asked, looking impatient.

"I think we need to recap everything again, update our board."

I was referring to the large board I had set up in the guest house to help us work through this problem.

"Can Becky come with us?" I asked Sylvie.

She waved a hand, and gestured she didn't have a problem. She hadn't said anything at all for a while.

"Sylvie, can you please do something for me?" I asked gently. "Make a list of who else was in the diner when Jordan and Jessica were having their dinner. I know it's been a while, but anything, or anyone you remember will be helpful."

"Okay, Meera. I'll do that."

The Christmas party was forgotten and we all got up to leave. Motee Ba decided to stay back at the diner just to be with Sylvie for a while.

Sylvie had started sobbing again.

"Thirty years we've been running this diner. But my food's never made anyone sick before."

The diner had emptied again and it wouldn't take long for the gossips to spread the word about Jon's arrest.

"Don't worry, Sylvie! We all know Jon's innocent. And he'll be out soon enough. You'll see."

We all hugged her as we filed out of the diner. Dad and Aunt Anita helped Pappa into the car and they went home. I got into my Camry with Tony and the others and we followed my Dad home.

Chapter 25

Lunch hour had already come and gone and my stomach rumbled as I parked my car in front of the guest house.

"I'm starving too," Jeet spoke up after a long time.

I asked Tony to update the board with what we had found out in the last two days. I decided to make a quick batch of grilled cheese sandwiches.

Becky broke open two cans of tomato soup and heated some up on the stove. I slathered thick slices of country bread with butter and grilled them until the cheese melted and began oozing out. We made short work of the food.

I had set some coffee brewing and we finally put our thinking caps on. The food had energized me and I was ready to tackle the problem with a fresh mind.

"How do you want to do this?" Tony asked.

"Let's list the main players, go over their story, and list any motives they may have had to harm Jordan."

"Do you want Stan here?" Becky asked.

I shook my head.

"There's a lot of information in my head right now. I want to make some sense out of it before I can present it to Stan. It will help if I can present it in a coherent manner."

"So let's do that," Tony said encouragingly.

"Who are the people in Jordan's immediate circle?"

Tony listed them out one by one.

"Pa Harris, Brother Cameron, Sister Pamela, Girl friend Jessica – I think that's the lot."

"Anyone else related to Jordan?" I pressed. "Aren't you

forgetting the ex?"

"What about Colin Stevens?" Tony asked.

I nodded. I drew a circle around Jordan and added the people closest to him.

"This is our first tier."

Then I added another circle and added 'Ex' whose name we didn't know. Then I also added Colin Stevens to the same circle.

"What about the people on the ranch, or anyone else he may have done business with?" Becky asked.

I drew a third circle around Jordan and added 'ranch hands', and 'business contacts' to it.

"Would Sylvie and Jon be in the third circle?" Tony mused. "They did interface with Jordan in some manner."

"Correct!" I added Jon and Sylvie's names into the third circle.

"We already know Jon and Sylvie are innocent, so let's strike their names out."

Tony's suggestion was approved and I drove a line through the Davises.

"I think we should start with the immediate family now," Becky spoke up. "Let's take Jordan's father first."

"Assuming that Jordan died from consuming nuts, I suppose everyone had the means to kill him." I looked at the others. "We can say that all of these people could easily have procured nuts. So no need to consider that point every time."

Tony and Becky nodded.

"According to Pa Harris, he was at the ranch all the time. But he was alone at the homestead. We don't know if he actually went out and came back any time."

I looked at Tony, inviting him to come up with a conflicting theory.

"Would anyone have seen him if he left the ranch?"

"I guess, but not necessary," I nodded.

I wrote 'Alibi' next to Pa Harris's name and listed it as 'Not Confirmed.'

"What would he gain by this?" Tony asked.

We had come to the all important motive. Did Pa Harris have any motive to do away with his favorite son?

"According to Pa Harris, the ranch was doing poorly until Jordan turned it around. He built the dude ranch business and made it successful. Every one of the family benefitted from this. So money certainly can't have been a motive here."

Becky spoke up.

"I can't imagine any other motive. Pa Harris seemed to be grieving for Jordan. That couldn't have been an act."

"He could've kicked Jordan out if there was any problem between them," Tony added. "No need to off him permanently."

"The only source of contention between them might have been Jordan's reconnecting with Jessica. Remember, he wasn't too pleased Jordan had broken his word to this other girl."

"So he could have lost face in the community, and blamed Jordan for it."

I looked uncertain.

"Sounds farfetched," Tony agreed, "but we are here to cover every possible angle. So write it down."

I made a note of it next to Pa's name.

"Let's move on to the next," Becky said, standing up to stretch her legs.

"Pamela Harris," I wrote on the board.

"Didn't you say she could have been here in Swan Creek?" Tony started.

"I thought so at first. But then she was apparently on a date. She was seen in some bar in another town, and then her date dropped her home. The police are convinced about her alibi."

"Could this date be lying?" Tony asked. "Maybe he had a hand in it?"

"That brings us to the motive," I frowned. "Pamela doesn't seem to be too emotional. She's never expressed any deep love for either of her brothers."

"You remember how she took our resort booking?" Tony asked. "That was barely two days after Jordan was found dead. So she was more interested in making a quick buck."

"Didn't you say she almost brought up the boys after their mother passed?" Becky spoke up.

"Right. She never went to college. Or got married. Maybe she harbors some resentment against Jordan for her lost youth."

I looked questioningly at the other two.

"That would apply to both her brothers, not just Jordan," Tony objected.

"How serious is she about this beau of hers?" Becky asked.

"We don't know that," I shrugged.

"What about money? Pam must be a co-owner of the ranch along with her brothers. With Jordan gone, anything from the ranch is split two ways instead of three."

"Jordan was the one who turned the ranch around, remember?" I put in. "Without him, it's just a piece of land. I don't think Cameron has the skills to run the whole ranching operation and keep it profitable. At least, not right away."

"They could sell it, I suppose," Tony said.

I shook my head. I had remembered my meeting with Cam.

"Pa Harris doesn't think much about women inheriting anything. He thinks Pam needs her brothers to take care of her. And Cam actually owns the ranch."

Tony and Becky stared at me.

"You never mentioned that before!"

"I just remembered," I told them, making a note of it on the board.

"That's one overwhelming thing in this whole business. There's just too much information floating around."

"So is resentment a strong enough motive?" Tony asked. "Apparently, Pam's not gaining any money out of this."

"She also seemed happy running the whole resort side of the ranch," Becky chimed in.

I wrote 'resentment' next to Pam's name as a possible motive.

"Don't they say revenge is best served cold?" I mused. "Do you think Pam's resentment could have built up over a period, up to a point where she just couldn't take it anymore?"

"Why was she hiding this beau from her family?" Becky demanded. "Maybe Jordan didn't like the guy and Pam didn't want anyone to come between her and her man."

"She could always elope, come on!" Tony rolled his eyes. "She's what, 45? She's not a child!"

"She's never really done anything on her own," I reminded Tony.

"What about Jessica? What if Pam didn't like her?" Becky asked.

"Then she would have harmed Jessica, right?" I asked. "I think hating Jordan for some unknown reason is the best we can come up with."

"Let's move on to the next one," Tony nodded.

"Cameron Harris," I wrote on the board next.

"The boys fought all the time according to Pamela," Becky reminded me.

"But Pa Harris said they've done that since they were kids. I don't think that means anything. Jeet fights with me all the time."

"Money sounds like the strongest motive," Tony said.

"I thought so too," I said to the other two. "But remember, the Triple H actually belongs to Cam. It's based on their grandfather's will. The oldest son gets it. Jordan was just working the land."

"What about the resort? Didn't Cam want to convert it into a home for wounded soldiers or something?" Tony asked me.

"He could've done it any time, since he owns the place. He did recognize the potential of the dude ranch business. He was willing to do both. Setting aside a few cabins for convalescent soldiers was good enough for him."

"Was there any other money involved?" Becky asked.

"I don't know. I guess Cam will also get some kind of pension once he retires. So he's in a good spot, as far as I know."

"Could they have fought over the girl?" Tony asked. "You did say he seemed kind of close to Jessica."

I thought for a minute.

"I talked to Jessica about that. I don't think she was interested in Cam. If you ask me, Cam was just playing around. Maybe he did flirt with her. But I don't think she reciprocated."

"So why did he do it?" Tony asked.

"I think he likes riling people up. He may have done it just to pester Jordan. The brothers could've fought over it."

"But in that case, Jordan would harm Cam, not the other way around."

Becky was right.

"What if he just couldn't stand seeing Jordan happy, for whatever reason. Could he have been jealous?" Tony asked next.

"Jealous enough to kill his own brother?" I shuddered. "I hope not."

I tried not to remember how besotted I had been by Cam's good looks.

I wrote Jealousy next to Cameron's name and placed a question mark against it.

"Have you noticed how Pa Harris lights up when he talks of Jordan?" Becky asked next. "Clearly, he was the favorite child. Maybe Cameron was angry over that."

I pointed to the board.

"That's jealousy again."

"What about Cameron's alibi?" Tony asked. "We know he was in Swan Creek. He slept over at Jessica's, didn't he?"

I nodded.

"That's not all. I think he even went to Willow Lake. Don't ask me why. But according to Colin, Jordan waved to his brother and spoke to him after Jessica left."

"So you mean Cam was present right there in the park after 8 at night?" Tony burst out. "Shouldn't you have mentioned that upfront, Meera?"

Becky joined in.

"So far, he's the only person who's actually been there on the spot. That makes him a suspect."

"I know he was on the spot," I agreed, "but what did he gain out of it? His motive doesn't seem strong enough?"

"Do you really think that, Meera?" Tony narrowed his eyes. "Or are you so smitten by that blue eyed jerk, you can't see straight?"

My mouth dropped open as I stared at Tony.

"What are you talking about? I don't care one bit about Cameron Harris. All I want to do is find the culprit, and bring Jon home by Christmas."

"Could've fooled me," Tony muttered.

Becky smacked him with a magazine.

"Enough of this nonsense. Stop acting like kids, you two."

Tony collapsed on a couch and put a cushion over his head.

"I'm taking a nap," he announced.

"I need fresh air!" I declared, ignoring him. "Wanna come walk around outside?" I asked Becky.

We bundled up, pulling on coats, gloves and scarves. We walked up to the edge of our property and into the lane. Then we turned back and went in the other direction.

"Don't you think Tony was being unfair?" I asked Becky.

She looked at me incredulously.

"You went out on a couple of dates with Cameron Harris. And you go on and on about how handsome he is. You didn't think it would affect Tony?"

"Affect him how? It's not like we are dating or anything."

"Meera, you can be so dumb," Becky shook her head. "And a wounded soldier. Who's ever measured up to that?"

I ignored Becky and took an interest in the bare branches of the trees surrounding us. Little icicles had formed, and there was a peculiar beauty in the stark landscape. I breathed in the cold air, and felt myself relax.

"Ready to go back in?" Becky asked after a few minutes.

"Yes. Let's finish what we're doing."

We walked back to the guest house, waving at Pappa standing in the living room window.

Chapter 26

I stepped into the kitchen to pick up some cookies for a snack. I was hoping I wouldn't run into my aunt. Back in the guest house, Becky had put on a fresh pot of coffee.

"Are you done sulking?" I asked Tony.

He didn't respond but he got up and went to the bathroom. Becky was pouring the coffee by the time he came back, looking freshly scrubbed.

Something about the smell of coffee signals my brain to snap into gear.

"So, we covered the three Harrises," Becky gave me the cue. "Who's next?"

"Jessica."

I wrote on the board.

"Isn't she Daddy's little girl?" Tony asked. "And she's got plenty of money."

"Money dries up like that on a research project," I said, snapping my fingers. "But we've established Jordan didn't actually have any money."

"Did they truly love each other? What about the time when they broke up?" Becky reminded me.

"I think she's more focused on her research. Jordan wanted to get married years ago but Jessica said no. That's why they broke up."

"What if all this was an elaborate plan? He dumped her the first time, so she wanted revenge."

Tony put forth a revenge based idea again.

"You mean she pretended to hook up with Jordan, got engaged, all for what? Just to get closer to him and ... and what?"

I shook my head.

"I can see Jessica making a fool out of Jordan just to laugh at him, or teach him a lesson. But I don't see her killing Jordan for it."

"It could have been a spur of the moment thing," Becky suggested. "Didn't they have a fight that night?"

"I talked to Jessica about it," I told them. "She wanted to move down south to her Daddy's place. Jordan didn't want to leave the Triple H."

"One of them would have needed to back down," Tony observed.

"Or break up," Becky finished.

"So once again, doesn't seem like enough of a motive to take a life."

"So we have a big fat question mark in place of motive," Tony said, frustrated.

I put the question mark in front of Jessica's name. I did that to remember we had considered the question, just hadn't found anything substantial.

"What about being in the area, or having the opportunity?" Tony asked. "Jessica looks the best for this."

"She was with him in the diner, of course," Becky counted on her fingers. "She knew he was allergic to nuts. And she was with him in the park too. She could easily have doctored the pie."

"That means nothing if she didn't have a motive," I protested.

We were quiet for a while, thinking about what we may have missed.

"Let's move on to that other guy – Colin Stevens," Tony said, rubbing his eyes.

Becky let out a yawn and that set us all off.

"We can't afford to take a break. Who knows what Jon is going through right now."

I reminded them of the gravity of the situation.

Tony and Becky tried to look alert as I wrote Colin's name on the board.

"What's the motive here, Meera?"

"Colin is clearly besotted by Jessica. They used to be engaged but Jessica dumped him when she rekindled her relationship with Connor."

"He can't have liked that," Becky bobbed her head. "Does he look like the type to bear a grudge?"

"Sure does! And he keeps bragging about how Jessica tells him everything. He knows a lot about Jessica, although I suspect most of it is because he listens in on her calls."

"What a weasel," Tony said in disgust.

"He's happy now that Jordan is out of the picture. He hasn't bothered to hide it."

I remembered how pleased Colin had been that Jordan was no longer in the picture.

"So he could have done it to get Jessica back."

I thought of how repulsive Colin was. Was that reason enough to believe he could kill someone? Then I remembered how cool he was about the whole thing. He hadn't even expressed any remorse over losing Jordan. So maybe he was capable of the crime.

I wrote Jessica next to Colin's name.

"So now we need to know if he could have done it," Becky continued.

"The answer to that is Yes, I guess," Tony looked at me. "Wasn't he right there in the park?"

I nodded in agreement.

"He went to the park around 8. And he was alone with Jordan for some time. Jessica had gone to use the restroom that time. He said he saw Jordan taking the pie box out of the truck."

"So when did he poison the pie?" Becky asked. "Was he already at the truck when Jordan and Jessica got there?"

I tried to think back to our conversation.

"We only have their word about this. But according to Colin, Jordan was by his truck, and Jessica had gone to the restroom."

We were stumped again. I put a question mark next to Colin's name again.

"Seems like we are coming up with more questions than answers," I moaned.

"I think we eliminated quite a bit of scenarios, though," Becky tried to cheer me up.

"What if some of these people were acting together? That changes the picture drastically."

Tony stood up and stared at the board.

"Have you noticed one thing?" I asked Tony and Becky. "None of their alibis depend on each other. Except Colin and Jessica's of course. But they went back to her lab and were with plenty of other people."

"What about the person Colin saw Jordan talking to? His brother, supposedly?" Becky asked.

I had completely forgotten about that.

"Cam never mentioned it."

"Would you?" Becky asked.

"It makes him look guilty," I paused.

"Why don't you call and ask him?" Tony smirked. "Maybe he'll spill the beans, confess over the phone."

I ignored the sarcasm and dialed Cameron's number. He answered after a couple of rings.

"Hello Cam, how are you?" I started.

"Hey Meera!" his voice sounded perky as usual.

"They arrested one of our friends …" I began.

"We heard," Cam crowed. "Pa's happy they nailed him."

"But he's innocent!"

"Of course he will say that. Look, Meera, I know you've probably known the man for a long time. And I'm not saying he did it on purpose. But it could have been an accident."

I stayed firm.

"These people have been in the food business for decades. They wouldn't make this kind of mistake."

"Are you saying there is not even a tiny chance of error here?" Cam roared into the phone.

That made me pause. If I were being logical, I had to accept Cam's argument. I decided to steer him to the purpose of my call.

"Actually, I have a question for you."

"What is it?" he asked indulgently.

"Were you present at Willow Lake Park that night?"

There was silence at the other end.

I waited a few seconds and prompted him. "Cam?"

"Who told you that, Meera?" Cam asked flippantly.

"Someone claims to have seen you there, talking to Jordan. You didn't mention this before."

"I was there," Cam responded with a sigh.

"Why?"

"Jordan had mentioned they might be going to the lake after dinner. I had a few drinks at the bar. Then I thought I would go and talk to them."

"Even when you knew they were on a date?" I pressed. "A special date celebrating their engagement?"

Cam laughed. I could imagine a naughty, irreverent look on his face.

"That engagement was a farce, if you ask me."

"That's not the point, Cam. Did you do it just to irritate them?"

"Look, I don't know. Like I told you, I was pretty wasted. I don't remember why I did it. I was just driving around. There's nowhere much to go in that small town anyway."

I knew that part was right. Cam was still speaking.

"I walked around the lake, I think, trying to spot them. Then I saw them arguing. It was something silly like where to live after they got married. Then Jessica went off somewhere. And Jordan started talking to some other dude Jessica knows from college."

"What happened after that?"

"We talked for a while. He was pretty upset. He was shoveling pie in his mouth like he hadn't eaten in a month. That was one of the few weaknesses he had. Stress eating."

"Wait a minute. So you saw Jordan eat the pie that killed him. Why haven't you said anything about it all along?"

Cam was quiet.

"You know this doesn't put you in a favorable light," I told him.

"Why would I harm my own brother?" he asked me again.

"What happened after that?"

"He wanted to be alone. So I left and drove to Jessica's. I took the key and crashed at her place. Then I drove home in the morning."

"You need to tell all this to the police," I said urgently. "It will help them establish the time of death."

Cam was quiet.

"Do you think I was the last person to talk to Jordan?" he asked me.

"It's beginning to look that way, Cam," I said gently.

"I don't even remember much of what was said," he said, sounding bitter. "Nice big brother I have turned out to him. I was right there, but I couldn't protect him."

Nothing I said would have changed anything. I thanked Cam and hung up.

"I suppose you got all that?" I asked Tony and Becky.

"Most of it," they agreed.

"Cam's big on the theatrics. But I don't think he harmed Jordan."

I moved back to the board.

"So we were looking at this second circle," I started again.

"We know almost nothing about this woman," Becky pointed out. "But if anyone has a strong motive for revenge, it's her."

Tony and I both agreed.

"Wasn't Stan going to find out where she was?" Tony asked.

"The police are working on it, but no news on her yet. Maybe Stan's found something new today."

There was a knock on the door, and Motee Ba came in.

"You're back!"

I rushed to hug her and ushered her to a seat on the sofa.

"How's Sylvie?" I asked. "Is she feeling better now?"

"She cried her head off for hours. Reema took her home." Motee Ba looked at Tony. "I wanted to bring her here, but Anita's visiting. And I knew you kids would have turned the guest house into a war room of sorts."

She swept her arm around, and noticed the giant board. She stood up and read everything we had on there.

"Good work," she said, patting me on the shoulder.

"It's all beginning to run together now," I complained. "Nothing's making a lot of sense."

"Have you looked at the time?" Becky gasped.

None of us had noticed it was beyond 8 PM.

"No wonder I'm starving," Tony smiled.

"We've got some leftovers," Motee Ba said. "Why don't you kids order something? That way, you can continue working on this."

"Call Stan, Meera," Tony reminded me. "Ask him to come over for dinner."

We put in an order for a truck load of Chinese food. Motee Ba left and we all collapsed on the couch.

Stan agreed to come by. I switched on the TV, and we all agreed to suspend any talk of the case until Stan got there.

The food and Stan arrived at the same time.

"Let's eat first, please!" Tony begged.

I looked at Stan as I ladled Hunan Chicken onto my plate along with some Lo Mein. I grabbed a couple of Crab Rangoon.

Stan looked relieved.

"I'm exhausted. I need to eat first too, Meera."

Everyone loaded their plates. The next fifteen minutes were spent munching greasy Chinese food, washing it down with beer or soda.

Finally, I broke open a fortune cookie and read the cryptic message.

'We often ignore what's staring us in the face.'

"That's helpful!" I scowled, trashing the paper.

Tony loaded big bowls with ice cream and drenched it in chocolate sauce. We ate our ice cream, summoning the energy to tackle yet another big discussion.

The hour was late and the clock was ticking. We needed to pull ourselves together for Jon.

Chapter 27

"How's Jon holding up?" I asked Stan.

He shrugged, looking apologetic.

"As well as possible, under the circumstances."

"Do you think he did this on purpose?" Becky asked, sounding defensive.

"No one's saying that. We think it could be a case of negligence." He held up his hand as I opened my mouth. "It's possible, Meera. Think about it a bit. No one can be perfect."

Becky crossed her arms and looked away. Her mouth was set in a firm line. She worked at the diner so maybe she could be implicated too. I hadn't thought of that.

"Personally, I don't think anyone at the diner is responsible," Stan admitted. "But I have to do my job. The only way to get around this is to find out the real culprit."

I pointed to the board. At first glance it looked like a lot of chicken scratch on a giant white surface. You had to actually read everything to make sense of it. We were quiet as Stan went through all of it.

"Have you arrived at any conclusion yet?" he asked, looking around at each of us.

I shook my head.

"We haven't found anyone with a strong enough motive. And then, all of them seem to have good alibis. We placed Cam at the scene of the crime. But as unpredictable as he is, I don't think he did this."

"My money's on Colin Stevens," Tony told Stan.

"We haven't finished talking about the second circle yet," Becky reminded us.

"Jordan's ex. We know nothing about her." I looked at Stan hopefully. "Were you able to check on her, Stan?"

Stan smiled.

"I was coming to it. Eleanor Robinson checked herself out about six months ago."

"What do you mean, checked herself out?" I asked, shocked. "Wasn't she incarcerated in an asylum?"

"Incarcerated? No. And in an asylum? No."

Stan looked smug. I bet he was holding on to some vital information.

"What do you mean?" Becky burst out.

"We questioned a few people who lived in the area. Jordan and the girl were tight. She'd grown up on a ranch, in a very protected environment. She couldn't take it when Jordan dumped her for Jessica."

We had heard about this already.

"They had a fight and she slapped him, maybe scratched his face." Stan paused. "The Jordans, they made it look like she was mentally unstable. I don't know how that whole insane thing came into play. A local judge convinced her to go into a sanatorium type of place."

"We've heard all that before," I said impatiently.

"The point is," Stan stressed, "there were no actual charges filed. She went there voluntarily. And so she checked herself out of there voluntarily."

"Is she back at her ranch then? Someone would have seen her by now."

Stan sighed.

"They sold the ranch long ago. It was just her mother and her, anyway. We tried to find out if she mentioned her plans to anyone over at that sanatorium."

"And?" I asked, leaning forward on the edge of my seat.

"She may have gone to Dallas, but we haven't found her exact location yet."

Tony looked interested.

"That's not very far. She could be here in a few hours, any time she wanted to."

Stan agreed to that.

"Fact is, she hasn't come across as someone who would hold a grudge. She was a simple girl. Barely graduated high school. Spent her life on a ranch in a town smaller than ours."

"Jessica's definitely the smarter one then," Becky said. "I suppose she was more appealing to Jordan."

"Hello. Have you looked at Jessica?" Tony rolled his eyes. "Beauty and brains is an irresistible combination."

I ignored Tony. He had been getting on my nerves a lot.

"Are you continuing to look for this girl?" I asked Stan.

"We are. I am beginning to think she may have changed her name. There's not much of a trail."

"Do you have a photo?" I asked.

"We are waiting on one," Stan told me.

The photo reminded me of my age progression program. I hadn't talked to Stan about it yet.

"Stan, I have decided to reopen my mother's case," I began.

Stan looked surprised.

"But I thought …"

I wrung my hands, trying to swallow the bile that rose up in my throat.

"Well, yes, but I still want to find out what happened to her. Maybe some new information came to light after all these years."

"That's been known to happen," Stan nodded. "A lot of cold cases are being solved thanks to DNA evidence, or new advances in forensics."

"Ya, well," I nodded. "I am contacting different departments and trying to increase the search area. Since this is the place from where she went missing, I thought I should let the Swan Creek department know."

"You might need to send a formal email or letter," Stan said. "I'm not sure what the exact procedure is."

"I'll do whatever's needed. But I wanted to give you these first." I handed over the set of 10 photos I had printed out. "I can email you a digital image too. I'm doing that with other people."

"What's this?" Stan asked curiously.

I told Stan about the program I had written.

"This is a projection of what she might look like."

Stan gave me an admiring look.

"That's brilliant. I will put these on file right away."

I hesitated.

"Have you been able to trace that car?" I asked Stan.

I was finally beginning to believe someone was following me.

"I was coming to that," Stan said. "We ran the tags your aunt gave us. Turns out it's a rental car like we suspected. And this time, it's from a small local place."

The excitement in the room ramped up.

"So? You know who it was rented out to?" Tony rushed ahead.

Stan winced.

"Not really."

"How's that possible?" Becky groaned. "Doesn't the rental company have it on their record?"

Stan shook his head.

"It's not really a rental company. It's more of a garage. They are not very particular about their records. And they can look the other way if they get more money."

"So you mean this woman paid them to not write down her name?" I asked.

"Something of that sort," Stan shrugged. "They won't say exactly. I think someone took a cash payment, maybe a double payment, to keep this off the books."

"Now what?" Tony asked.

"We have told them to inform us whenever the car is returned. Hopefully, we will get there in time to talk to this person."

I slumped down on the couch and let out a yawn.

"We still haven't considered the third circle," Becky said in a tired voice.

"That's farfetched," Stan said, reading the board. "But it's been known to happen. It is almost impossible to find out unless someone speaks up."

We were talking about the ranch hands or any unknown person who may have wanted to harm Jordan.

"Let's call it a night," Tony said, getting up.

"I have to leave now, Meera," Stan stood up to leave too. "You have done a good job here. Let me know if you think of anything else."

Stan left and Tony and Becky collapsed on a couch.

"Why don't you guys stay over?" I asked. "That way, we can get an early start in the morning."

Tony and Becky readily agreed, each staking claim to a room in the guest house. I walked over to the main house and crept into my room. A hot shower helped me calm down a bit. I fell into a deep sleep which was thankfully not interrupted by any bad dreams.

Motee Ba was stirring a big pot of oatmeal when I walked into the kitchen the next morning. Becky and Tony were already munching on toast, guzzling coffee while waiting for the oatmeal. Pappa was tapping his cane, spooning his soft boiled egg into his mouth.

My Aunt Anita was quiet for a change, pouring sugar over her grapefruit.

The phone rang. It was Sylvie on the line for Motee Ba.

"How are you Sylvie? Are you at the diner?"

The cops hadn't shut down the diner this time, but Sylvie wasn't in good enough shape to run it. Becky waved her hand, trying to get my attention.

"Becky wants to know if we should go open the diner," I told Sylvie.

"I don't know, child. Who's going to turn up, anyway?"

"It will be fine, Sylvie," I tried to soothe her.

"Honey said y'all were working on finding out who killed that boy. Why don't you keep on doing that?"

"But what about the diner?" I asked.

I thought the diner would be a good distraction for Sylvie.

"It's not like the folks need me to be open anymore," Sylvie started.

People in small towns like Swan Creek depend on certain places. The diner was one such place. There weren't too many restaurants in town. And none of them were as economical as Sylvie's, or provided a down home menu that the locals depended on. It was the place you went to for your eggs and bacon in the morning, or your soup or sandwich for lunch. And it's the place you went to for a slice of pie. I wondered what the future was for Sylvie's, if Jon was convicted. I tried to steer myself away from worst case scenarios.

Sylvie had continued talking while I was lost in thought. There was a pause, and I realized she had asked me something.

"I'm sorry Sylvie, I didn't get that last part."

Sylvie sighed.

"I know you must be exhausted, Meera. And you're supposed to be on Christmas break."

"I'm fine, Sylvie," I tried to reassure her. "We'll have Jon home for Christmas, you'll see."

Sylvie let out another sigh.

"Now what were you saying?" I reminded her.

"Don't worry about the diner. And tell Becky the same thing. We'll let those Robinsons earn a buck or two."

Bells clanged in my head as something clicked.

"Who are the Robinsons?" I was almost afraid to ask.

"It's those two women from that fancy diner place!" I could almost see Sylvie shaking her head.

"You mean Nancy's?" I asked.

I wanted to be doubly sure.

"That's the one alright," Sylvie said, suddenly sounding tired.

"Sylvie?" My heart skipped a beat. "Do you remember I asked you to make a list of all the people in the diner the day Jordan and Jessica were there?"

"I have it," Sylvie confirmed. "Maybe Becky can add something to it. My memory's not that good anymore."

I coaxed her to tell me the names she had come up with. I wrote them down on the back of an envelope I found on a side table. Finally, I hung up, forgetting that Sylvie had called to talk to Motee Ba.

"I think she called for you, Motee Ba," I apologized. "I forgot."

"I'll call her back," Motee Ba smiled. "Don't worry."

I begged Jeet to help clear the dishes. I hurried over to the guest house with Tony and Becky following me. They had picked up on my excitement.

"Spill it, Meera," Tony said, as soon as we entered the guest house. "What did you find out?"

"I don't want to jump to conclusions."

I handed over the envelope to Becky.

"These are the people that were present at Sylvie's when Jordan and Jessica were having their celebratory dinner. Can you think of anyone she might have missed?"

Becky skimmed her eyes over the paper. She checked off the names I had written down one by one.

"I don't remember some of these. But if Sylvie wrote them down, they were there."

"I know that," I cut her off. "Was there anyone she missed?"

"Well, I was in and out of the kitchen," Becky began.

Her eyes had a faraway look in them. I knew she was thinking hard. Becky handled both the cooking and the serving a lot of the time. Most customers spent at least fifteen minutes in the diner, even if they were only there for coffee. So my guess was Becky would come across every customer at least once.

"I think this accounts for most people sitting on the bar stools. But there was someone at the last table, the one close to the rest rooms. I think there were two women sitting there."

"Do you remember who they were?" I asked.

Becky shook her head.

"Maybe they weren't regulars. Generally, I remember people. Most people come in at a certain time and order the same thing."

I didn't want to prompt Becky any further. I had a hunch but I wanted Becky to confirm something on her own.

Tony got a call on his cell phone.

"Meera, I think I'll have to put in a few hours at the gas station," Tony said apologetically. "There's a big delivery coming in. It's my last one before the new year."

"Go!" I waved him off. "Nothing much happening here anyway."

"Maybe I should go be with Sylvie for a while," Becky said.

"Good idea!"

I took a deep breath after saying goodbye to Becky and Tony. I placed a call to Stan. It was time to find out if my hunch had any substance.

Chapter 28

Stan sounded tired on the phone.

"Good Morning, Meera!"

"What did you say that girl's name was? The one Jordan dumped?" I asked him.

"Eleanor Robinson?" Stan asked.

"Do you know there's a mother daughter duo by the name of Robinson in town?"

Stan listened with mounting excitement as I shared what I was thinking.

"You think that's possible?" he asked eagerly.

"Can you find out if these are the same people?" I asked.

"I'll get on it right away. Check county records etc. They must have had to provide some papers somewhere if they are living in the area."

"How long will that take?" I asked eagerly.

"Can't say. Most offices will close later today. Staff is already on vacation."

"So you're saying you may not be able to confirm her identity for a while?"

Stan was quiet. I assumed he was thinking of an alternative.

"We may be able to speed things up if someone identifies her for us."

"You think Jessica might do that?" I asked eagerly. "Or Pamela?"

"I can't promise you anything," Stan said reluctantly. "But if someone identifies this girl as Jordan's ex, we can at least keep an eye on her."

"Okay, I'll get on it." I hung up, feeling a burst of energy.

After a moment's thought, I decided to approach Pamela first. Pamela must have met the girl several times.

Pam answered the phone. I didn't want to show all my cards at once, so I asked her if she would come to Swan Creek and meet me for some coffee.

"But why? Is there a reason you want to see me? It's a long drive, you know. And we've got some guests coming in today."

"Just trust me on this one," I coaxed.

Pam reluctantly agreed to meet me at Sylvie's.

I drove to Sylvie's guessing I would find Becky there. I was right. Both Becky and Sylvie were in the kitchen, rolling some cookie dough.

"Just trying to keep busy," Sylvie said.

"That's good."

I helped them decorate the cookies, adding red and green glitter on some. Most of my help consisted of sampling the different types.

"These are delicious," I exclaimed.

I heard a car drive up and went outside. Pamela got out of a truck. She wasn't looking too pleasant.

"So why have you called me here, Meera?" she snapped.

"Let's go to that new place over there," I pointed to Nancy's. "I hear they have good coffee."

Pam muttered something but she followed me as I crossed the road. Nancy's fancy diner was almost bursting at the seams. As expected, most of the locals had given Sylvie's a wide berth once again. It looked like all of Swan Creek had congregated at Nancy's.

We got a small table for two, near swinging doors that led into the kitchen.

I asked for two cups of coffee and waited.

"Why are we here?" Pam asked.

"Just enjoy your coffee, Pam," I smiled. "And be patient. Maybe you'll meet someone you know."

Pam gave up on asking me any more questions. She read through the menu and ordered some cake.

"This is good!"

She moaned as she enjoyed her chocolate cake.

"Our chef went to culinary school," the server said. "Unlike the cooks at other places in the area."

"Can we give our compliments to the chef?" I asked politely.

"I'll let her know," the server nodded.

The chef came out a few minutes later, her face wreathed in smiles.

"You like the chocolate cake?" she beamed. "It's six layers with real chocolate ganache."

Pamela's eyes widened, and she jabbed a finger at the chef. She swallowed the large bite of cake in her mouth and gulped.

"What're you doing here?" she cried.

Nancy Robinson had come out of the kitchen. She froze when she saw Pam. She leveled a dirty look at me.

"You are not welcome here," she told Pamela in a steely voice.

"See them out!" she ordered the server who was standing at one side, looking confused.

"Nellie! What are you doing here?" Pamela finally found her voice. "Why aren't you in your mental asylum?"

She stood and looked around, as if trying to capture the crowd's attention. There was no need for that because every eye in the diner was riveted on the scene playing out.

"This woman is insane!"

"Mama!" Nellie Robinson had turned red, and snot rolled down her nose.

"It's her. It's her, Mama."

Nellie sniffled and started sobbing.

"Get out!" Nancy screamed at us again.

I crossed my fingers, hoping someone had called 911 by now.

Nellie curled her fists and launched herself at Pam. Pamela's face lost its smirk. I stared at them in shock.

"Do something!" I screamed at Nancy.

Sirens blared as two police cars swung into the parking lot. Stan Miller rushed in, followed by four cops.

A couple of the diner staff had managed to pry Nellie away from Pam. She was coughing, and bruise lines were appearing on her throat where Nellie had choked her.

"Didn't I say, she's insane!" Pam croaked.

Stan's eyes met mine but he didn't say anything.

The police took Nellie away, and I took Pamela's arm. We crossed the road over to Sylvie's.

"What were you thinking, Meera?" Pam screamed. "Are you mad too?"

Pam had figured out why I took her into Nancy's.

I was shook up myself. I hadn't expected the girl to turn so violent. Then I realized how foolish I had been. I suspected the woman was a murderer. Of course she was bound to be dangerous.

"I'm so sorry," I rubbed Pam on the back. "I had no idea she would turn so violent."

Becky and Sylvie were staring at us, trying to be patient.

"We need to get you to the doctor," Becky said, handing over a glass of iced water to Pam. "You need to get that checked out."

Pamela looked at me. I owed her an explanation.

"We know Jon is innocent," I began. "We thought a lot about who might have wanted to harm Jordan. His ex was a possibility but you said she was in an asylum. Then we learnt she wasn't there anymore. I had a hunch but I needed someone to confirm it was her."

"We still don't know she did it," Pam said sadly.

"The police will make her talk," I said confidently.

"She's wily. She won't own up to it."

Becky and I took Pam to the ER. They gave her some pills and advised her to rest. I offered to drive her home to the Triple H. It was the least I could do. Becky drove my car and I drove Pam's truck. We dropped her off at the ranch and started back immediately.

Becky kept peering in the side mirror and almost opened her mouth a few times.

I held up my hand before she said a word.

"Please! I don't care if anyone is following us. I can't handle it right now."

Becky nodded, patting me on the shoulder.

"Do you think that girl did it?" she asked quietly.

"I can imagine her doing it," I shuddered. "You should've been there. One minute she was crying, and the next she just flew at Pam's throat."

We pulled into Sylvie's lot. I had a headache and it was probably from hunger. I was hoping Sylvie would have something ready for us to eat.

I parked the car near the diner door and Becky beat me to it.

"Sylvie, we're starving ..." she called out and stopped in her tracks.

I almost bumped into her. Then I looked up.

Nancy Robinson was pacing the floor. Sylvie was sitting at a table, looking worried. She seemed relieved to see us.

"They're here," she said.

Nancy Robinson clasped my hands tightly.

"She didn't do anything. She's innocent."

I wasn't so sure about that.

"I saw her attack Pam myself."

"I'm not talking about that," Nancy dismissed. "I'm talking about Jordan!"

"But didn't she attack Jordan earlier too? Wasn't that why she was sent to that asylum."

"For the first and last time, my daughter wasn't in an asylum!" Nancy shrieked and I took a step back.

Nancy collapsed in a chair and tried to hold back her tears.

"My Nellie was such a sweet girl. She was deeply in love with Jordan Harris. They were supposed to get married."

I nodded. We knew all about that.

"Jordan met this other girl one time, and then he just stopped talking to Nellie."

"Weren't they going to get married?" I asked.

Nancy grimaced.

"The wedding was planned. Nellie had her dream wedding dress. The invitations were sent out. All this time, that boy was seeing this other girl, and he didn't even tell us the wedding was off."

I wondered why Jordan had behaved like that.

"Nellie saw him with the girl, and asked him who she was. Then they broke up."

"Is that when your daughter attacked him?" I probed.

"It was nothing. She just lost her temper."

I had just seen a live example of Nellie's temper. I wondered if Nancy was guilty too.

Nancy spoke with a casual air.

"I promised to take her to counseling so no charges were pressed. She spent some time in that place. It was like a five star resort, with bars on the windows and locks on the doors. She did some fancy cooking diploma in Dallas. She was ready for a fresh start."

"Why did you choose Swan Creek?" I asked. "Didn't you know Jessica lived here?"

Nancy shook her head.

"Jordan got his degree a long time ago. He had been running the ranch for a few years when he was engaged to my Nellie. We knew this girl was from down South, but we didn't know anything else."

"Were you shocked when you came across Jordan here?" I asked.

Nancy was quiet.

"We spruced up the place over yonder. Nellie was excited. She had big plans for it. We had big plans. We came here for some coffee. Imagine her shock when she saw Jordan sitting there, holding hands with that girl."

"So she flipped and took her revenge," I stated bluntly.

"She did no such thing!" Nancy almost screamed in my face.

She stood up abruptly and walked out.

I looked at Becky and Sylvie. They hadn't spoken a word but their shocked expressions told me what they were thinking.

Becky spoke first.

"You remember the two women I told you about?"

I nodded. I had been waiting for Becky to connect the dots.

"I'm almost sure it was them – Nancy and her daughter."

"Were they here when Jordan got that extra pie?" I asked eagerly.

"Right there," Becky pointed to a table at the back.

"Does this mean they will let Jon go?" Sylvie asked eagerly.

"I don't know!" I tried to not raise her hopes too high. "It all depends on what Nellie admits to."

Becky was quiet.

"Do you really think she did it?"

Sylvie stood up and went into the kitchen. She shuffled out a while later with a big tray.

"Why don't you kids eat something first?" she said.

We attacked the chicken salad sandwiches Sylvie had brought out, and slurped the soup. I coaxed Sylvie to eat with us.

"What do we do now?" Sylvie asked.

I placed a call to Stan and listened for a while.

"Pam has pressed charges for assault. So they will be keeping Nellie for a while. Stan said they will try to get a confession from her."

I looked at Sylvie.

"I'm sorry Sylvie, but looks like they'll keep Jon there for a while. But he's doing well. They are taking care of him."

"Why don't we close this place up?" Becky suggested.

"Let's go watch a movie or something."

We drove to our place with Sylvie. Aunt Reema and Motee Ba came out when they heard my car in the driveway. We told them what had happened.

They all went inside. Becky and I went to the guest house. Tony and Jeet were sprawled on a couch each, watching an action movie. Becky told them the story this time and the boys high fived me.

"We don't know if she's guilty," I said glumly.

"I say she is," Tony insisted.

We all felt the same. The question was, how were the police going to prove it?

Chapter 29

We chose a Christmas movie to get into the mood. A couple of hours later, Jeet and Tony were pretending to yawn their heads off.

We were all a bit peckish, so we went into the main house to scrounge for food. Motee Ba was at the stove, frying *pakoras*. The kitchen was infused with the smell of the fritters.

"What kind are you making, Granny?" Tony asked, picking one up and popping it in his mouth.

"Onion *pakoras!*" Motee Ba announced. "And cheese if you want them."

I eagerly cut cheese into 2 inch cubes and handed it over to Motee Ba. She dipped the cubes into thick seasoned batter and dropped them in hot oil.

I took over the frying from Motee Ba and we gorged on the hot fried snacks, dunked in ketchup and washed down with hot tea.

"Where's Sylvie?" Becky asked. "Is she still here?"

"I convinced her to take a nap," Motee Ba said softly. "Any news from Stan?"

I shook my head. We went back to the guest house and slaved through one more movie, this time one chosen by the boys.

The phone rang around 9 PM. It was Motee Ba, calling us over for dinner.

We started walking out when a couple of cars pulled up in the driveway. One of them was a squad car and one was an unmarked sedan. They didn't have sirens or lights on. I crossed my fingers, hoping it was Stan with some good news.

My face lit up when I saw Jon get out of one of the cars. I ran over and threw my arms around him.

"They let you go? Thank God!"

Becky followed with a hug.

"Let's go in, Meera," Stan urged, shivering in the cold.

Everyone had rushed to the front door when they heard the cars and they were all filing out of our front door. Stan herded them in.

We sat in our living room, eager to get an update from Stan.

Sylvie sat close to Jon, her hand held tightly in his. She was looking lively for the first time since the last few days.

"Have you dropped the charges against Jon?" Dad asked Stan.

"Yes, we have, Professor."

"You should never have arrested him in the first place," Pappa put in his two cents.

"I agree," Stan said apologetically. "We needed to make an arrest at the time. And Jon and Sylvie were the obvious choice."

Jon looked around at everyone.

"I'm fine. Don't worry about me now. Listen to what he's going to say."

"Did she do it?" I burst out.

Stan's face told me the answer even before he said a word.

"Yes. She did. And she confessed to every bit of it."

"I suppose she'll get off this time too?" I said bitterly.

"It won't be that easy," Stan said. "First of all, there's nothing wrong with her mental state. The place she was in was more of a rehab place. She's just got a short temper, and she's malicious."

Stan looked uncomfortable.

"I can't reveal what went on in the interrogation. Let's say we suggested she may have been seen at the crime scene. That was enough to make her sing."

I remembered what Nancy had said earlier that afternoon.

"Was it all part of the plan then, coming to Swan Creek?"

"I don't think so," Stan said. "How much do you know so far?"

I gave everyone a quick recap of Jordan's connection to Nellie. Then I told them what Nancy had said earlier today when she came over.

Stan was thoughtful.

"I think it's possible Eleanor or Nellie remembered where Jordan used to go to college. And she may have known Jessica lived here. We'll never know for sure."

"What does she say? Was it all just a coincidence?" Tony asked impatiently.

"Nellie's story matches her mother's in this part. She spent a few months in that fancy clinic. Got her head straightened out. Then the two women went to Dallas where Nellie did some kind of food course. They wanted to move to a new place, start over. They had already sold the ranch, so they had money to invest. Swan Creek is one of the best places to live in America. They thought it would be familiar, since they were from the same state and all. Nellie said it looked like the place had potential."

"Potential to meet Jordan again, you mean," Becky smirked.

I tapped Becky on the shoulder and signaled Stan to continue.

"They found an ideal place for their restaurant, spruced up the place and were ready to go in business. They came into Sylvie's to check out the competition."

"And instead, ran into Jordan."

I tried to imagine what Nellie must have felt, how shocked she might have been to see her nemesis right in front of her, just when she thought she was making a new start.

"As luck would have it, Jordan and Jessica were celebrating their engagement. It was too much for Nellie."

"Did she ever intend to harm Jessica?" I asked. "She's the one who took Jordan away from her, so Nellie should've been mad at her too."

"We asked her that," Stan nodded. "But Nellie thought the fault lay with Jordan. He would've fallen for some other girl if not Jessica. He was the bad apple."

"Did Nancy know Nellie had spotted Jordan?" Tony asked.

I had wondered about the same thing.

"Maybe she did, but she didn't want to mention it." Stan shrugged. "It seems neither of them mentioned it to each other."

"How did she manage to mess up my pie?" Sylvie spoke up.

She had been following the conversation closely.

"Nellie heard Jordan order the extra pie. And she heard someone assure Jordan it was his special order. That's when she hatched her plan."

"Nancy said they went home afterwards."

Stan sighed.

"Nellie heard the couple mention the lake. She sneaked out and went to Willow Lake. She had crushed some pecans into a fine powder and put them in a Ziploc bag."

A hush fell over as we all realized the significance of Nellie's action.

"Nellie found Jordan's truck in the parking lot. It was open. She pulled the pie out of the box, sprinkled the powdered nuts over it and sealed it again. Then she just hid somewhere."

"She actually waited there?" I asked, aghast.

"We are hoping one of the surveillance cameras caught her."

Stan sounded as disgusted as we were feeling.

"She saw the whole thing. She saw Jessica and Jordan arguing. Then Colin came and picked up Jessica. Then Cam appeared and Jordan took the pie and followed him. She watched as he devoured the pie. Then she drove home and went to sleep."

"Did she know it was likely to be fatal?" Sylvie voiced the question at the top of everyone's minds.

"She just wanted to teach him a lesson," Stan said. "That's all she keeps saying."

We thanked Stan for bringing Jon over and bid him good night.

There was a hush over the group. Sylvie came over and hugged me.

"You said you'd have him back before Christmas and you did, Meera. How can we ever thank you enough?"

"I had a lot of help," I smiled, putting an arm around Becky and Tony.

"All that's fine, girl, but what about my dinner?" Pappa grumbled, tapping his cane. "Have you looked at the time?"

Dad poured Scotch and wine and we toasted Jon and Sylvie.

The lights on the Christmas tree twinkled and there was a festive atmosphere in the house for the first time in the season.

Tony, Becky and Jeet dragged me into my room.

"You were awesome, Meera!" Tony's eyes shone as he looked at me.

"Please, I couldn't have done it without you. I think we just stumbled onto it by luck."

"Not really," Jeet said seriously. "The police didn't even know about Jordan's first engagement until you found out about it. You explored options, examined them and eliminated them. I think you had a logical approach."

"Okay, Einstein," I ruffled his head affectionately. "You can hire me to investigate your cases when you become a hotshot lawyer."

That set off a discussion about Jeet's college admission.

I slept in the next day, exhausted by the whole episode. I sat in the kitchen, enjoying my breakfast after a long time. Motee Ba had made my favorite cheesy scrambled eggs with jalapenos. I mixed in some salsa into my eggs and scooped them up with a cheese quesadilla.

"Where's everyone else?" I asked her.

"Your aunt's gone shopping with Reema. Pappa and Dad are at the barber's. Jeet's hanging out with friends."

I wondered what Tony was up to. I thought of the gift I had got for him and wondered if it was enough.

Motee Ba smiled at me.

"He's going to love it."

I blushed.

"I don't know what you mean."

I said a quick prayer for having Motee Ba in my life. That reminded me of the other project I had taken up. The decision to look for Mom had been mine but the outcome was going to affect everyone.

Motee Ba ladled the rest of the eggs on to my plate.

"Becky said a car was following you yesterday too."

I nodded.

"She said that. But I'm not sure myself."

"Have you been in any scrapes recently?" Motee Ba asked me.

"What? Of course not!"

"Then why would someone follow you around, Meera?"

"Beats me. If they want something, they should just come forth and talk to me, right?"

The phone rang as if on cue.

"It's for you, Meera."

Motee Ba handed me the receiver. I leaned back in the kitchen chair, twisting the long telephone cord around my finger.

"What's up, Stan?" I asked, spearing another forkful of eggs and salsa.

Stan had news for me.

"The car was returned," he began. "It was a woman alright. She switched cars and drove off."

"Did you question her?" I asked eagerly.

"We missed her! We are short staffed, Meera. Today's Christmas Eve."

I sighed.

"Becky thinks she spotted a tail yesterday."

"Maybe that's why the woman switched cars," Stan said. "We have a general description, and we have the tags. We are just waiting for her to speed or run a light or something so we can pull her over. But she's very careful."

"Can't you do anything else?" I asked, frustrated.

I had been dealing with this ghost for the whole semester and I was finally beginning to lose it. I just wanted to confront whoever it was, and ask them what they wanted from me.

"Normally, a rental place copies the driver's license for records," Stan sounded as frustrated as I did. "But this place hasn't done that. I may try something different though. One of my nieces is pretty good at portraits. I am going to take her to this rental place."

"You mean get her to draw a sketch of that woman?" I was

getting excited.

I was impressed with Stan Miller. The old Stan was a paper pusher who didn't think much beyond putting in his hours. But Stan was turning over a new leaf.

"Let me know if you find out something," I told him.

I went into the living room with an armful of presents. I placed them around the tree. Then I rearranged all the presents a bit so they looked pretty. Motee Ba clapped as she looked on from her favorite chair. I went and perched on the arm, placing an arm around Motee Ba.

"It's perfect, Meera," Motee Ba said softly, snuggling into my shoulder.

I remembered what Motee Ba had always taught us, growing up. Life is as perfect as you want it to be. So we had a few challenges ahead of us. But the Patels of Swan Creek, Oklahoma had a lot to be thankful for this Christmas.

Thank You

Thank you for taking the time to read A Pocket Full of Pie.

If you enjoyed the book, please consider leaving a review.

I would also really appreciate it if you tell your friends and family about the book. Word of mouth is an author's best friend, and it will be of immense help to me. Your efforts are much appreciated.

Thanks!

Author Leena Clover

Leenaclover@gmail.com

http://twitter.com/leenaclover

https://www.facebook.com/meerapatelcozymystery

Join my Newsletter

Get access to exclusive bonus content, sneak peeks, giveaways and much more. Also get a chance to join my exclusive ARC group, the people who get first dibs at all my new books.

Sign up at the following link and join the fun.

Click here → **http://www.subscribepage.com/leenaclovernl**

Books in the Meera Patel Mystery Series

Book 1 – **Gone with the Wings**

Book 2 - **A Pocket full of Pie**

Book 3 - **For a Few Dumplings more**

Book 4 – Back to the Fajitas

Keep reading for Meera's yummy recipes like Mutton Curry, a glossary of Gujarati/ Indian terms and a sneak peek into Book 3.

Glossary

Desi – broadly refers to people from the Indian subcontinent

Gujarati – of the Indian state of Gujarat; pertaining to people from the western Indian state of Gujarat

Ba – Mother

Motee Ba – Grandma, literally Big Ma – pronounced with a hard T like in T-shirt

Thepla – a flatbread made with wheat flour, pan fried. Chopped fenugreek leaves are often added to the dough along with spices like turmeric and coriander.

Kem Cho - how are you; standard Gujarati greeting

Khichdi – stew made with equal quantity of rice and moong dal lentils

Kadhi – buttermilk stew thickened with gram flour, seasoned with Indian spices

Samosa – fried pastry triangles stuffed with veggies or meat

Pakora – fritters, generally vegetables dipped in batter and deep fried

Sneak Peek – For a few Dumplings more – Book 3

Heavy black clouds hung low on the horizon. Winter winds buffeted everything in sight. The weather forecast gave ample warning of a cold front coming in. I wanted to get home before the roads turned icy. My old car wasn't the most reliable in bad weather. A healthy hum of conversation rippled through the diner. The hardy folk of Swan Creek had bundled up and chosen to spend Saturday afternoon at Sylvie's Café and Diner. Many of them didn't have a choice if they wanted a hot meal.

Most of the local women were attending one of the most important meetings of WOSCO, the local ladies' club. The Women of Swan Creek Oklahoma or the WOSCO Club has been around since World War II, and they believe in keeping busy.

Becky topped up someone's coffee and rubbed her lower back with her other hand. I motioned her to come and sit down at the small table wedged between the kitchen door and the pantry.

"I swear, if I pour one more coffee today ..." Becky blew out a huge breath and dabbed her forehead with a napkin.

It might be 40F outside, but the blast of hot air coming out of an overhead vent wasn't doing us any favors. We had been at it since breakfast, and with Sylvie gone, we were rushed off our feet.

I had barely touched my tushie down when the phone rang. Jon held up a hand from the counter as I started to get up. Two soup bowls full of Jon's spicy gumbo were calling to us. I couldn't wait to start eating.

"Just two of these left?" Becky grumbled, pointing to the *samosa* dumplings on a plate.

"There's plenty of stuffing left," I reassured her. "We'll fry us some more after we take a break."

The samosa dumplings are the latest item I have added to Sylvie's menu. Samosas are pastry triangles stuffed with a spiced potato mixture, deep fried until golden. They are a very popular Indian snack, even in small town Oklahoma. I had mixed some chicken in, making them even more popular.

We had fried up a few dozen for the WOSCO meeting. A couple dozen had been gobbled up by the weekend crowd.

Jon walked up to us, shaking his head.

"That was Sylvie. They want a couple dozen more of those dumplings."

I swallowed my first spoonful of gumbo and stared at Jon in dismay.

"What, right now?"

Jon nodded.

"Those women sure must be hungry. Sylvie said their meeting hasn't started yet. It will easily go on for 2-3 hours more."

"I'm not getting up until I eat this," Becky declared. "I'm dead on my feet."

We scraped off every bit of the gumbo from our bowls, guzzled our colas and finally got up.

"I'll do the frying," Becky offered. "I still can't fold them as well as you."

I rolled out the dough in circles, stuffed the dumplings and Becky fried them up. Soon we had a couple dozen ready to go.

"Want to ride with me?" I asked Becky.

"I wish," she groaned. "One of us needs to be here to help Jon."

I covered the tray of dumplings with a lace doily and placed it on the front seat of my battered Camry. I drove out slowly, taking the straightest possible route to the Lucas house. Lucas mansion, really.

The local ladies come up with a calendar of activities for the year, including everything from charity to pure entertainment. The annual election of the club was coming up, and the first meeting of the year is always an important one. This is where the women throw their bonnets into the ring. I mean, put in their names to be on the committee. Motee Ba, my grandma, is an active member, and so is Sylvie. Motee Ba had been hinting that she wanted to run for President. Sylvie supported her and was eager to be her running mate. Personally, I wasn't sure my grandma would be able to usurp Mary Beth Arlington, the sitting President of the last ten years.

The Lucas kid was lurking by the garage when I pulled up to their front door. Their acreage is even more lavish than ours, which meant I could park anywhere I wanted. I stooped in to pull out the tray, feeling eyes on my back. Teenagers!

The kid smirked when I caught him staring.

"Don't you have school or something?" I glared.

"Saturday," he grinned.

I acted cool, ignoring him, and walked up the steps to their front door. Balancing the tray in one hand, I lifted my hand to knock. There was a healthy buzz of voices inside. A groan went up and someone swore. The voices rose a few seconds later, until a scream rent the air.

I gave up any thoughts of being polite and banged on the door. I doubted anyone could hear it in the uproar. Someone pulled open the door suddenly, and walked into me.

"Meera!" Henry Robinson gasped, staring at me wildly.

"What's the matter, Miss Robinson? I heard a scream."

A scream wasn't that unusual in a big gathering of women. But my Motee Ba was inside, and I wanted to make sure she was fine.

Henry Robinson remained tongue tied. I gently nudged her aside and entered the spacious foyer. A wide flight of stairs led to the second floor landing. I followed the voices to a room a few paces to the left. All the women were gathered around something, buzzing like bees.

I placed my tray of dumplings on a side table and sidled up to the women. I put my hand on someone's shoulder and tried to peer through. I wasn't ready for the sight that met my eye. A frumpy old woman lay motionless on the floor. She was wearing a navy dress that had seen too many washes. The scarf lying beside her had cost more than her entire outfit. One hand held a crushed samosa dumpling while the other was wrapped around the leg of a table.

"Is she...?" I looked around, trying to spot my grandma.

The wail of sirens sort of answered my questions.

Can't wait to read on? Get your copy of For a Few Dumplings More!

Keep reading for Meera's yummy recipes!

RECIPE - Black Bean Burger

Ingredients

2 cans black beans

½ tsp garlic powder

½ tsp onion powder

¼ cup green peppers, diced fine

¼ cup red peppers, diced fine

¼ cup sweet corn

1 jalapeno pepper, diced

¼ cup scallions, diced fine

½ tsp Ancho chili powder

½ tsp cumin, ground

1 tsp sweet paprika

1 cup+ breadcrumbs

Method

Wash and drain the black beans until dry. Add to food processor. Add the seasonings and spices and pulse until minced.

Transfer black bean mince to a bowl.

Add the diced/ chopped peppers, scallions, chili etc.

Add salt only at the last minute before cooking the burgers.

Add in half the bread crumbs and mix. Add more breadcrumbs as needed later.

Refrigerate patty mix for half an hour or more.

Apply some water or oil to your hands and form patties.

Cook them on a hot grill, a few minutes on each side.

Add a slice of pepperjack cheese or cheese of choice on top of the patty.

To serve the burger

Squirt chipotle sour cream on one bun. Apply guacamole on the other bun.

Place patty on the bun.

Add sliced onion, tomato, lettuce etc.

Add pickled jalapenos and salsa.

Add some tortilla chips.

Place the bun with the guacamole on top.

Fiesta Black Bean Burger is ready to be served.

RECIPE - Mutton Rogan Josh Curry

Ingredients

250 g mutton cubes (lamb)

4 Tbsp ghee or clarified butter

4 pods green cardamom

4 cloves

1 inch cinnamon stick

1 tsp fennel seeds, crushed

2 bay leaf

1 Tbsp ginger, grated

1 large onion, slivered

½ cup plain yogurt

1 tsp Kashmiri chili powder or paprika

1 drop Kewra water

Salt to taste

Method

Add half the ghee to a thick bottomed pan or wok.

Fry the onions until brown. Remove with a slotted spoon and set aside.

Add the remaining ghee to the pot.

Add whole spices to the ghee and fry until aromatic and the cardamom pods split open. This can take a few seconds depending on how hot the ghee is.

Add the meat and fry for about 10 minutes until any fat is rendered.

Add the yogurt and fry until the yogurt dries up and is absorbed.

Now add onions and chili powder and fry for a minute.

Add one cup of water and the grated ginger. Add salt per taste.

Simmer on low heat for 10 minutes or more until meat is tender.

Add a drop of Kewra water or Kewra essence (optional). Be very careful with this since it is quite potent.

Serve with Naan or rice.

RECIPE – Cheesy Jalapeno eggs

Ingredients

6 large eggs

1 Tbsp sour cream

1 Tbsp butter

½ jalapeno pepper, deseeded and chopped fine

½ cup shredded cheese

Method

Crack eggs into bowl. Add a splash of water and sour cream and whisk until frothy.

Add a knob of butter to a pan.

As butter begins to melt, add in the jalapeno pepper. Fry until the pepper sizzles a bit and becomes aromatic.

Pour the whisked eggs into the pan.

Cook slowly on low heat, stirring occasionally.

Add in the cheese as eggs begin to set and switch off the heat.

Fold lightly a couple of times before serving.

RECIPE – Orange Tequila Grilled Chicken

Ingredients

4-6 boneless skinless chicken breasts

4 cloves garlic, crushed

1 cup orange juice

1 tsp orange zest

30-60 ml tequila

¼ cup olive oil

½ tsp dried oregano

½ tsp cumin, ground

½ tsp chili seasoning or

1-2 chipotles in adobo

1 Tbsp brown sugar

Salt to taste

Method

Marinate chicken breasts with all the ingredients for 4-6 hours or overnight.

Place the chicken breasts on hot grill and cook about 10-12 minutes on each side until done.

Serve with fresh lime and orange wedges and sides.

RECIPE - Cheese Pakora Fritters

Ingredients

8 ounce processed cheese/ mozzarella cheese

1 cup gram flour

¼ tsp turmeric, ground

Pinch of cayenne pepper

¼ tsp carom seeds or *Ajwain*

½ tsp baking soda

Pinch of baking powder

Salt to taste

Oil for deep frying

Method

Whisk all the flour and spices together. Add half a cup of water and more if needed to get a thick pancake like batter.

Add in the baking powder and set aside for 10 minutes. Add baking soda just before you are ready to fry the fritters.

Cube any hard cheese of choice. You can cut it in squares or sticks – any shape you want.

Heat oil in a wok for frying. When the oil is hot enough, you are ready to fry the pakora fritters.

Dip a piece of cheese in the batter, coat well and drop it in the hot oil. Fry for a few seconds until it puffs up slightly and becomes light brown. Use slotted spoon to transfer to plate.

Repeat the process for the rest of the cheese.

Serve cheese pakoras hot with ketchup or chili sauce.

Note – Batter should be thick enough to coat cheese. It should not fall off otherwise cheese will melt in the hot oil.